Gangsters

Evan Zimroth

Dead, Dinner, or Naked (poetry)

Giselle Considers Her Future (poetry)

Gangsters

A Novel

Evan Zimroth

Crown Publishers, Inc.
New York

Copyright © 1996 by Evan Zimroth

Published by Crown Publishers, Inc., 201 East 50th Street, New York, New York 10022. Member of the Crown Publishing Group.

Random House, Inc. New York, Toronto, London, Sydney, Auckland

http://www.randomhouse.com/

CROWN is a trademark of Crown Publishers, Inc.

Printed in the United States of America

Library of Congress Cataloging in Publication Data is available upon request

ISBN 0-517-70309-2

10   9   8   7   6   5   4   3   2   1

First Edition

For my sister,

Lisa Spector

ברוך אתה יהוה אלהינו מלך העולם,
הגומל לחיבים טובות, שגמלני כל-טוב.

Blessed are you, Lord our God,
King of the universe, who bestows
good things upon the guilty, who has
bestowed every goodness upon me.

—From the Hebrew liturgy

(Part 1)

(in the beginning)

The secret truth about Tom and Nicole is that when they fell in love they didn't know each other at all.

They hadn't even known each other's names at that moment when their lives sheered off into love, but it didn't matter in the least. Not because they had no identity, far from it, but because they were so stripped, so pared down, so exposed to each other. Because at times each one felt that merely to be looked at, gazed upon, by the other was to give up everything; even sitting side by side without saying a word told the other person everything hidden and secret. When they stripped each other's bodies, too, it wasn't only for some ephemeral pleasure: it was to find something out, to uncover and reveal what was hidden. Also, to leave a mark. Especially in the apartment.

In the Jewish tradition, you are named after a relative who has died; you are never given the name of someone still living. It is considered insulting, or maybe even lethal, to name a child after someone alive. It is as if you wished that person dead. But Nicole, even though she was Jewish, was not named after a dead relative. Rather, her father named her after Nicole Diver in *Tender Is the Night*, his favorite novel. And Tom—who knows about Tom? Tom could just simply have named himself, *ex nihilo*, out of nothing, in the same way that he sometimes leaned on an expensive, silver-tipped cane. For nothing, to make a certain kind of impression. For panache.

So their names weren't really important. What mattered was that they became inextricably bound up in each other.

Perhaps they didn't especially want this process to happen, perhaps they might have been happier had it not happened, but they could not evade it. In fact, after a while Nicole even accelerated it. She simply threw herself into the whirlwind. When they first met, Tom had said to her, "You are going to feel as if you've been run over by a twelve-ton truck. Please tell me when you start feeling that way. And I will try to pull back. I can't promise you I'll succeed, but I'll try. Because it really will feel to you like a truck."

When Nicole heard that warning, she was delighted— in fact, she was exultant. And grateful. What she felt like saying to Tom, but didn't yet dare to say, was, "I want you to give up everything and come and live with me forever. Because I love you." But she couldn't say that to him, not then, because he was a stranger. He was a stranger, even though she suddenly felt she knew him thoroughly. And she still was a stranger to him.

Tom looked so earnest, telling her he would mow her

down like a truck. So what she said to him, out loud, was, "That's okay. What I haven't told you is that I've always wanted to throw myself under a truck." She meant it, too. In fact, you might say Nicole had spent her life looking for the largest, heaviest, most beautiful, and most dangerous truck. It wasn't getting run over by a truck that would scare her, it was the part about pulling back. So their names were the least of it. What matters is that they were chained.

(outside, evening)

Nevertheless, Nicole was skittish: yes, she was in love with him, but she had no idea what to make of him, no idea of what she was in for. He was charming and attractive in a clean-cut, Presbyterian sort of way, that much was evident, but she really knew very little about him. Not where he lived, or how he survived, or where his romantic affections might lie. If anywhere. There was something gentle and diffident in his manner, but something mocking as well, so from the beginning she didn't quite trust him.

The first evening they had a meal together, Tom had asked her an odd question. *Who had hurt her the most?* They were barely into conversation when he asked her that. It was a violation, she thought, but also nakedly inviting. The way Tom asked his question disarmed her: he sat back in his chair abruptly, with a look on his face as if he might get slapped for asking. Something about maybe hitting him made Nicole want to answer, almost in spite of herself, to tell him who it was and why and how it had happened, but suddenly she couldn't say a word. Instead she started to cry.

She didn't cry much, really. After all, they were in a restaurant, and she did not especially want to be noticed or stared at. She just wept silently for a moment and then pulled herself back together. She saw how ridiculous, how absurd, she was to cry, even for a second, and suddenly she was quite buoyant again. Good Lord, she thought, let him provide his own awful stories, his own etiology of pain. So she batted the same question back to him: What about you, who has hurt you the most?

Tom was willing to answer, though. It was someone whom he had been wildly in love with and wanted to marry. Someone he had moved heaven and earth to be with. At the last moment, the woman bailed out. It made him desperate. He prowled the streets every night, afraid to go home, afraid to be alone. He was so lonely he could taste it, like a disk in his throat; he was choking on loneliness. He would get drunk and telephone her, he threatened to kill himself. But it didn't work; she was gone. He himself had put her into a taxi, like a gentleman, off to wherever, somewhere without him. It takes two people to start something, Tom pointed out, but only one to end it. Later, years later, he couldn't remember why he had been so insanely in love. But there you are. Love isn't pleasant, it doesn't make the world go 'round. It doesn't even make you happy, we all know that. It makes you want to kill yourself, he said. Doesn't it.

They were signaling to each other somehow, the way people do, in some fragile, intangible way that's barely recordable, as if the invisible shifting of one molecule were to start a chain reaction. As if only one subtle, minute shift could start a landslide or the upheaving of a mountain range. What one would think happens gradually over centuries occurs sometimes in a fraction of a second. There is a microfissure somewhere and the landscape utterly changes. Tom and Nicole both felt it. If at that moment they had been better friends, if they had known each other at all, they could have described the shift, that signaling to each other.

Later he gave her words for it: "My heart swerved," he would say. But that was later. For now, they felt it and didn't talk about it. His heart had swerved, and so had hers. Silently.

(outside, evening)

This is where I live," Nicole said, nodding in the direction of the entry to a medium-size Manhattan apartment building. She hesitated, not quite sure yet whether to go home or stay out a few extra minutes.

"Do you have to go in yet?" Tom asked. "It's still early."

"I do," she explained, "I have car pool tomorrow morning."

"Car pool," he repeated gravely, as if Nicole were telling him that upon arising in the morning, she would perform an exotic rite. Tom was clearly unfamiliar with the rigorous life called forth by small children in Manhattan.

Nicole laughed at the puzzled look on Tom's face. She told him that her two kids went to the Thackeray School on the other side of town, so she and other Thackeray parents car-pooled them back and forth. Tomorrow morning, Tuesday, was her turn, when she would board her own kids into her green Volvo station wagon and then pick up four more children en route. On Wednesday afternoons she reversed the process, picking the children up at school and dropping them off at their homes. After her stint of morning car pool, she would head back to the Upper West Side, garage her car, come home, clear the breakfast dishes, start the laundry, make beds, plan dinner, go off to the university where she taught a morning class, hold office hours . . .

But for a moment Nicole forgot about car pool and dinner and laundry. She remembered only that they had been together in a restaurant, that he had made her cry, and that he had wanted to kill himself over a woman who had ditched him. She remembered what he had said about love, that it was hardly ever full of joy, that it quickly spilled over into anguish. Finally she just let out a long, deep breath and then, for no reason at all, she said, "Please."

He waited, but she was silent. In the night air, she shivered slightly but didn't yet turn away from him. Finally she gestured vaguely toward the front door of her building. "I'd better go in," she said. "I really do have to get up early."

"Before you go," Tom interrupted, "I have to tell you something."

It was her turn to wait quietly while he gathered his thoughts to tell her he would mow her down like a twelve-ton truck. In those few moments she silently ordered herself to look at him carefully, to be pitiless, to see all of his flaws, because it was her last chance to see him as he really was. It all passed in a fraction of a second, but she tried to notice everything about him that was unappealing or in some way unsatisfactory. But even as she, in seconds, cataloged everything that she might not like, Nicole knew it was hopeless. I'll see it all again, she thought to herself, I'll see him clearly, but only when I'm no longer in love with him. Clarity was impossible. Time was running out, time already had run out. After that moment, the way she saw Tom would be through the prism of her love.

Even though he was threatening to mow her down, to run her over, he started to laugh. He looked suddenly like the happiest man on the face of the earth. She laughed, too.

"That's okay," Nicole answered jauntily. "What I haven't told you is that I've always wanted to throw myself under a truck."

She meant it, too. They were laughing, both of them, but she knew she could just as easily be crying. Tom, too, probably. That's the funny thing about laughing, that it can be so much like crying. That it can be full of sobbing and confusion. So she was dangerously close to tears. At this point, maybe they should have said good night, but they didn't say anything at all and just looked at each other for a second or two. After that, they said good night.

(at the window)

It was true, Nicole had been run over by a twelve-ton truck. Not, of course, without her volition. If you position yourself in the middle of a highway and wave down a truck, you are likely to get run over. That's what falling in love is like: you post yourself wherever the greatest danger is. You know, with certainty, that in the long run there is only devastation and loss. But you do it anyway. You fall in love, whatever the stakes.

The first time Nicole fell in love, she was five years old. It was with an older boy, someone named Scott, who was seven. He was the first bad boy she had ever met, so Nicole was mesmerized from the beginning. She didn't *like* him; he wasn't at all likable; but she fell in love with him the first night they met. It had been a summer romance, all distance and impossibility, but it had left its mark on her. Like many such romances, Nicole's love affair with Scott took place at a resort, a summer colony beside a lake where Nicole had been taken by her grandparents.

In the afternoons her grandparents played pinochle or mah-jongg with their friends, while Nicole lay on the grass next to their card table, amusing herself with an extra deck of cards and listening in a desultory way to the adults. In between hands they taught her how to play solitaire and gin rummy; they passed her pretzels and handed her celery tonic in a glass bottle. They also tried to make her play with Scott, but without success. She actually loathed Scott: he was spindly and unattractive and couldn't even swim. When the two children and the grownups left their cards to pitch horseshoes before dinner, he couldn't throw as far as Nicole. Nicole detested him. But every night she fell in love with him all over again.

At dusk, about nine o'clock at high summer, Nicole and Scott were both put to bed by their grandparents. Her room was on the third floor and Scott's directly overhead. Her grandmother would put her in a nightgown, then tuck her into bed, kiss her good night, and leave the room, in a hurry to get back to the card table on the lawn. Nicole loved that moment when she was finally alone.

Her cot was right by the window. She could gaze out into the dusk, feeling that special edge of loneliness when you are in bed and you know that you will never in a million years be tired enough to sleep. So she would lie there, waiting for her grandmother to go downstairs and disappear. She was listening for Scott.

In a few minutes, there would be Scott's voice, calling her from the window of his room.

"Are you there?" he would call out. She knew he would be leaning out his window, searching for her. Nicole would come to her own window, put her elbows on the sill. She would look out into the darkness.

"Yes, are you?"

"Are you in bed?"

"Yes," Nicole would say. She meant yes, she was in bed, and yes, she was alone, and yes, she was waiting for him.

"Do you want to play?" he would ask, directing his question out into the night air. Nicole wouldn't answer. Of course she wanted to play. She waited for him to call out again. There would be silence for a few moments. Then, Scott's voice again.

"Say shit."

"Shit," Nicole would call back up to him.

"Say fuck."

"Fuck."

She sat quietly at the open window, not moving. When she wanted to, she could lean out and look up, and there would be Scott, leaning out of his window and calling down to her. She didn't really want to look at him, though. It was enough to hear his voice.

"Say cock."

"Cock."

"Say motherfucker."

"Motherfucker."

"Say cunt."

"Cunt."

"Say asshole."

"Asshole."

"Say cocksucker."

"Cocksucker."

It was slowly getting darker, the air more and more fragrant. In the distance, in the quiet, Nicole could hear crickets and, far below her window, the sounds of grown-ups, laughing and talking. *Motherfucker,* she would call out to Scott. *Cocksucker. Asshole.*

(the Wolfes' apartment, morning)

Caroline, Nicole's eleven-year-old, was in the foyer of the Wolfes' large apartment, piling up her books neatly on the floor and then sliding them into her backpack. "Mom!" she called out. "Where's my poem about the starfish at the beach? Did you remember to type it?"

"On the dining room table," Nicole answered as she came into the foyer from the kitchen, holding two lunch-boxes and pushing her unbrushed hair out of her eyes. When her son, Jake, skidded by, Nicole managed to collar him for a second. "Change—your—shirt," she said as the six-year-old slipped out of her grasp. "Jacob! You cannot wear a dirty shirt," Nicole called after him as he dashed into his room. "You need to . . ." Her voice trailed off.

When the children had reassembled and were zipping up jackets, gathering backpacks, and swinging them over their shoulders, she hovered around, keeping them moving toward the door and school. Their father suddenly appeared in the middle of this little crowd; he, too, was sailing off for the day, carrying his briefcase, grabbing his jacket. "Elevator," he said as everyone spilled out into the hallway. "Did someone push the elevator button?"

The elevator door opened. Nicole gave each child a last kiss and shepherded them into the elevator while her husband held the door. "Good-bye," she said to everyone in general. "Have a good day, all of you. Bye, kids. Bye, David. See you later." She stepped away from the elevator.

David, keeping one hand on the elevator door so it wouldn't close on his children, leaned over toward his wife. "Good-bye," he said to her under his breath, "asshole." He stepped back into the elevator and the door closed.

(inside again)

Back in her empty apartment, Nicole leaned against the door. She looked blank, not upset, not angry, just blank and washed out. It was as if someone had hit her so hard that she was numb, beyond pain. She rested for a moment, looking nowhere.

When she moved it was slow, like walking underwater, but pensive and mechanical. She had tasks to do. She made Caroline's bed, threw a quilt over Jake's. She made the bed she shared with David, arranged the pillows. In the kitchen she cleared the breakfast dishes from the table, stacking them carefully in the sink, running cold water over them. She squeezed out a sponge and wiped it across the table. Then she took a load of laundry out of the dryer, dropped the clothes onto the table, and began to fold. She folded the children's underwear, her husband's T-shirts, their clean pajamas, and the towels. She shook the things out, matched the edges, carefully pressed out creases with the palm of her hand. She made a little pile of everyone's socks, and when she came across a matching pair she folded that, too, doubling them over and turning down the cuffs.

The telephone rang.

Nicole paused a moment in her folding but otherwise did not move. She just looked blank, while the phone rang and rang, six times, eight times, ten times. The phone stopped ringing, finally. But then, a moment later, the ringing started again. Nicole was still immobile, as if she were stone deaf. After the sixth or seventh ring, she finally picked up the receiver. She held it away from herself for a second, still deciding whether or not to answer. "Hello," she finally said. Her voice was dull, without expression.

"Hi, honey!" It was David's voice at the other end. "I just got in—where were you? How come you didn't pick up?"

Nicole said flatly that she was folding laundry.

"Yeah, well . . . Anyway, you should see the stack of things on my desk! How about you? Got any plans?"

Nicole was silent for a moment. "Um, uh," she mumbled. "Uh . . . not exactly—what I mean is—I have to teach—and write a lecture . . . Look, David, how can you—"

"Great! I'm sure you'll be terrific, but what I need from you now is—"

"What?" Nicole asked warily.

"You could do me a great favor, a really big favor. My shirts. If you could just pick them up from the Chinese. I have this big meeting tomorrow, first thing. You know, on that teen mothers thing. But I need my shirts. It won't take you more than a minute—"

"Shirts?" Nicole asked as if nothing made any sense. "Where are they?"

"I told you, at the Chinese."

"But I don't have the ticket. You need a laundry ticket."

"No problem," David reassured her. "It's on top of my dresser. Or maybe in my top drawer. Possibly in the pocket of my gray-and-black tweed jacket, or one of the other jackets in my closet. The inside pocket, I would guess—"

"What you mean is, you lost the ticket."

"Don't worry. Try the places I mentioned, and anyway, you don't really need the ticket. Just tell them it's number two-D. *Two-D*. Got that?"

Silence from Nicole.

"You are a sweetheart! Just terrific! Now, honey, I've got to hang up. People are lining up outside my door."

"Will you be home for dinner?"

"I'll try, I really will. Can't tell how long my late meeting will last. Don't wait for me. Bye, honey. Good luck with your lecture. Tell the kids I'll take them out for ice cream when I get home. Or whatever. But don't wait. Bye."

Nicole put down the receiver. She was pensive, still.

Then she picked up the telephone again. She dialed a number, waited a moment to hear one ring, and then hung up. Right away Nicole's phone rang.

Hello, Nicole said quietly, answering the phone. *Yes, it was me. I have until nine-fifteen. Are we on?*

(after the flood)

The telephone was ringing again as Nicole left her apartment, but this time she really paid no attention. She had quickly showered and changed from her jeans and T-shirt to a loose skirt and pullover sweater, to panty hose and low-heeled shoes. With her hair finally brushed, jacket on, briefcase in hand, she was all set to go to work.

She taught in the Department of Comparative Literature at the local university where she had gone to graduate school; even after her marriage she had continued to live in the neighborhood and could easily walk to work. Her office, on the fourth floor of an imposing but decrepit building called Marbridge, was down the hall from her old friend Jules, her colleague and confidant. Each semester she taught a survey course, sometimes in tandem with Jules, on either the Bible or Great Books of the Western Tradition. Most recently she had been lecturing on the Bible, the family narratives in Genesis, those cycles of slaughter and misdirected love. More than the stories, though, she thought she understood the mania of the Bible: God sends a flood to devastate the earth, wipe everything out, but suddenly, lo!—dry land. Never mind that the next thing you see is one solitary man, poor Noah, lying naked and drunk, absolutely blotto, on the ground. Nicole moved quickly. She was about to find a little piece of dry land herself.

"Two coffees," she said to the woman behind the counter of the deli on Broadway. "One regular, one black.

Sweet'n Low on the side." The man she was about to visit expected her to bring coffee if she came early in the morning. And to wear a full skirt that he could lift easily so he could take her quickly, sometimes even standing up, both of them fully dressed, not even bothering to lie down on the couch. Sometimes, if they spoke briefly on the phone before they met, he told her to remove her underwear before she came. She always complied, and he always pleased her; she even loved him a little. But she never told anyone about him, especially not Jules, who tended to watch her like a hawk and suspect the worst.

Several blocks away she turned a corner, entered another apartment building, larger and more impersonal than her own and inhabited by offices as well as by families. Without having to search, she pressed a button on the board in the entry. When an answering buzz unlocked the front door, she crossed the lobby and rang a doorbell on the ground floor. The door opened, and Nicole handed her paper bag to the man inside. Then the door closed behind them.

The man checked the coffees, chose his, stirred Sweet'n Low into it with a wooden stick.

"No Danish?" He sounded amused.

"This is your basic no-frills fuck," Nicole replied, sipping her coffee.

"You said nine-fifteen, didn't you? Let's see"—checking his watch—"that gives us twelve minutes."

Nicole put down her coffee and began to peel off her sweater. She grinned. "What will we do with the other eight?" she asked.

(the campus)

That was the day she first met Tom, that afternoon, with Jules.

Jules and Tom were walking together across the campus, talking man to man. Both carried briefcases, both were dressed almost identically in a formal, academic style, in ties and heavy tweed sports jackets. But otherwise they could hardly be mistaken for each other. Tom, for one thing, used a cane or perhaps it was a walking stick, an elegant object with a silver knob at the top. It was a stage prop for him, something he could lean on, ever so lightly. Not that he seemed wounded, or lame, or anything of the sort that required aid; he could just as easily wave it in the air or point with it as lean on it. The cane was an old story. He had used it for years, ever since he had first arrived in New York. Jules, of course, wouldn't have been caught dead with something as effete as a walking stick. He was darker than Tom, heavier, morose and sardonic, whereas there was something quick and flickering, something stagy, about Tom. And the cane did make him seem a little forlorn, even when you knew that it was just to make an impression that he carried it.

While the two men were talking, Nicole rode toward them on her bicycle, cycling slowly to dodge small children, strollers, pedestrians on the crowded walkway at the university. She was wearing the same loose skirt, sweater, short jacket, and low-heeled shoes that she had worn in the morning; her briefcase was hooked over her left handlebar. A parcel wrapped in brown paper was jammed into her bike basket; it just might have been a package of shirts from the Chinese laundry. As she reached the two men, she dragged both feet along the sidewalk to come to a slow stop in front of them.

"Did you call me this morning?" she asked Jules, not bothering to say hello. "My phone was ringing as I left, and I had a feeling it might be you."

"No," Jules said curtly, "I haven't called you for a while. I've probably forgotten your number, actually. Maybe you should give it to me again, just in case."

"Never mind." Nicole got back on her bicycle and began to pedal very slowly. She circled around the two men, pedaling with one foot and dragging the other along the pavement. As she circled, Tom and Jules had to rotate to talk to her. Jules indeed had some news: he wanted Nicole to know how important his companion was. "Architect to the stars," he began, "the Pritzker, *Time* magazine's cover, remember? There was that documentary about him." Nicole circled slowly on her bike; she was used to Jules's enthusiasms. "But fame is fleeting, right, Tom?" Jules continued, turning to his companion. "How's your wife, by the way? Gotten over that motorcycle business yet?" Tom leaned a bit more heavily on his cane and shrugged, almost imperceptibly, when Nicole finally looked at him, as if for the first time.

"Not a motorcycle. A car," he said with a wry smile at Nicole. "It wasn't me, anyway. It was my evil twin brother."

Nicole continued to size him up. But Jules hardly caught the interruption and carried on in a rush. They had met after Jules's lecture on postmodernism and the Old Testament. "Hundreds of people there," Jules reminded Nicole, not for the first time. Who knows, Jules went on as if he'd just thought of it, who can tell the ways of God? Maybe this is Tom's road to Damascus. Maybe . . .

"Don't believe a word of it," Tom warned Nicole, who was still pedaling slowly, listening to Jules. "I have no work, that's all. Architecture studios tend to collapse under lawsuits. Not to mention the architect responsible." He tried his nonchalant smile again, but it turned into more of a grimace.

Nicole nodded and put both feet down to stop her bicycle altogether so that she could look more closely at Tom, this earnest stranger who was derelict, close to folding. Tom reddened; he looked discomfited, trapped. His wry self-effacement and hint of secret terror gave Nicole an unexpected jolt: she suddenly wanted to kneecap him—to stun him again, without mercy—and, simultaneously, to provide comfort and solace. But all she said was that she knew what he meant about collapse; it sounded familiar.

"I talk to lawyers," Tom confided, "and insurance people. All day. So I cheer myself up reading about plagues and floods and murders of the firstborn. Since I have no work. And maybe won't, ever again."

Nicole grinned. " 'From him who hath not,' " she quoted, " 'more is taken away.' "

Tom looked surprised for a second and then threw back his head and laughed.

"You can say that again," he agreed fervently. "I'm like you people," he continued. "Wandering in the desert. Longing for the fleshpots I left behind."

"Was it good?" asked Nicole intently. "Your Egypt, I mean?"

"A lot of it was," Tom answered. "And I want it again."

"You okay?" Jules asked Nicole, seizing the conversation that had quickly excluded him. "Get your daily quota of manna yet?"

"I don't know," Nicole answered, sounding suddenly weary and getting back on her bike. "David and I had a huge fight last night—"

"Ma nishtanah?" Jules cut in in Hebrew with a rhetorical flourish. "So, why is this night different from all other nights?"

"Do you people *always* quote Scripture?" Tom asked, directing his question to Nicole and rotating with her as she circled again. "I thought only *my* people—"

"We don't call it Scripture," Nicole began primly. "And anyway—"

"And with this kind of talk," continued Tom, "we sometimes do a little laying-on of hands. Safe sex."

Nicole smiled. "Have to get going," she confided to Tom as if she were talking to a good friend whom she would see again later. "I promised to meet some students in my office before my kids get home from school." She nodded to the two men and pedaled off, expertly balancing her briefcase.

(the campus)

Who was that?" Tom asked, no longer leaning on his walking stick but drawing circles with it in the air as if he were still watching a woman circle around him. "I didn't catch her name."

"You don't want to know her," Jules answered darkly. "We're colleagues, she has an office down the hall from me. A boring woman, if you ask me, boring and—"

"She didn't seem so boring," protested Tom, keeping his eyes on Nicole as she cycled down the path. "Who is she?"

"—boring *and* dangerous," continued Jules. "In a disastrous marriage. Has countless affairs. She lies incessantly, just for the hell of it. I'm doing you a favor—"

"She looks perfectly benign to me," Tom said. "She's got a job, kids, a fancy Italian bike—"

"Very dangerous," Jules said.

"Hmmm, you could be right," said Tom judiciously. "I noticed she was wearing an ankle bracelet." He watched carefully until Nicole was out of sight.

(the Wolfes' bedroom)

That night David came into the bedroom he shared with Nicole. It was late; the children had been in bed for hours. Nicole, in a T-shirt and panties, was propped up on her pillows, reading, a quilt thrown loosely over her. David walked in quickly, taking off his jacket and yanking at his tie, pulling them off and throwing them over a chair as he talked. "Hey, you're still up," he said with a big smile. "I thought you'd have turned out your light long ago. Everything all right? Kids okay? Did Caroline tell you I called—that I'd be late? By the way, you picked up my shirts?"

"As long as you don't suddenly appear when I'm putting the kids to bed," mumbled Nicole, continuing to read. "You always make such a racket. Takes forever to get everyone settled down." Then she added, "Yes, I got your shirts."

"Want to know what happened?" David asked. "The meeting was great! I had those guys eating out of the palm of my hand. By the end they were practically throwing money at me. So it's a green light on teen mothers. Even you liked the script, you must admit."

"Mmmm," Nicole murmured, not looking up.

"Can't you say hello?"

"Hello."

"Nice of you to look up and say hello."

"I said hello. How many times do I have to say it? *Hello.*"

"What are you reading?" David came over to the bed and tried to peer into Nicole's book.

"Nothing," said Nicole, rolling over in bed so that her back was to her husband. She propped herself up on one elbow, her head in her hand. "I'm just reading, is all."

"Yeah, but what? I mean, I come home after being at

work all day, one meeting after another, I just put together this terrific deal, and you can't even say hello. So at least tell me what's so absorbing that you can't even look up from your book."

Nicole closed her book and looked up at David, pained. "I'm reading Lévinas, if you must know," she said slowly and deliberately. "His essays on the Talmud. A chapter about when God turns Mount Sinai upside-down over the Israelites and threatens to drop it on their heads if they don't accept the Torah."

"You do find the kinkiest stories, don't you," David said suspiciously, but trying to maintain his good mood. "We didn't read that in yeshiva."

"Obviously."

"Hey, now wait a minute," David protested. "It was a great yeshiva. Maybe not up to *your* standards, but a great place."

Nicole nodded in agreement, so David pressed his luck. "Would you like to come into the kitchen and have a cup of tea with me?"

"No," said Nicole, "I'm reading, remember? But you go ahead."

"I thought you said you were almost finished."

"Then I'm going to read the Lands' End catalog. I could use a skirt. Then I'm going to sleep."

"From the Lands' End catalog?" David exploded. "Can't you do any better than that? Haven't you ever heard of Madison Avenue? Bloomingdale's?"

"Too busy," Nicole snapped. "You think all I have to do is shop for clothes?"

"Well, a little shopping won't hurt you. I mean, the stuff you buy from catalogs looks like, well, you know, like it came from a catalog."

Nicole ostentatiously returned to her book. "Look," she said, "I don't bother you when you're reading. . . ."

"I'm not bothering you!" David shouted again. "I'm just talking to you. You're my wife, remember? I come home—after a grueling day—and you don't even say hello."

"Hello. For the nineteenth time."

"Would you like me to bring you some tea?"

"No, thank you."

"Some orange juice?"

"No."

"A peanut-butter-and-jelly sandwich? Remember, in the old days, when you used to wake me up in the middle of the night and make me eat sandwiches with you? Remember?"

"No."

"You don't even remember peanut butter and jelly?" David asked, terribly hurt. "How could you have forgotten?"

"I don't mean I can't remember. Of course I remember that," answered Nicole wearily. "But I don't want any now. I want to read. If you will just excuse me . . ."

"Maybe a yogurt?" David continued hopefully, leaning over the bed and patting Nicole's backside.

"I'm not hungry, thank you, and you don't need to pat me. I'm fine, thank you."

"Okay, okay," David answered genially. "I get the message. You're not hungry, you just want to read." He continued to pat his wife, leaning over her, rearranging the quilt. "Here—you're going to be cold," he said, pulling up the covers. "I'll just cover you, and then I promise—"

"Get out!" yelled Nicole suddenly, jerking herself away from him and throwing the covers down. "Get the fuck out, will you! Let me read, for God's sake!"

(a phone booth)

Nicole left her apartment house early the next morning, just as soon as her children left for school. She went directly to the public phone booth on the corner, fished in her jacket pocket for a quarter, and dialed. After a moment she hung up, but instead of walking away she just stood still. A moment later the phone rang and Nicole picked it up. She spoke briefly, nodded, and then hung up for the second time. As she quickly left the phone booth and took off down the street, she happened to glance into the corner café and there was Tom, watching her through the large window. Tom's glance immediately caught hers; it was as if he had been watching her the whole time. He was with a group of people, but he might just as well have been alone, waiting for her to step into that phone booth and make her call. Watching her receive a call in return.

As their glances locked for a second, Tom rose from his chair. Just as swiftly, he caught himself and sat down. Nicole walked by without even nodding. But she had seen the gesture, had seen Tom nearly leap out of his chair and then think better of it. She knew he had been watching her all along. So that's the way it is, Nicole thought. He knows, and I know.

If the finger of God points in your direction, there is nothing you can do to withstand it. Divine providence makes you fall in love, and divine providence removes love from you, utterly and without consolation. You can dodge all you like, you can even in your own way plead and beg, but to no avail. When Moses marched up the mountainside where he would die without ever having made it to the promised land, the unfairness of it didn't move God in the least. All the wailing and moaning of the Israelites didn't make God relent for an instant, so Moses died, hale and hearty at the age of one hundred and twenty, the promised land still just a glimmer in his eyes. Sometimes you glimpse the promised land from a telephone booth, where suddenly you look up and your future is there before you, in all its pain and glory.

A block or two later, Nicole stopped and picked up two coffees, one regular and one black. Sweet'n Low on the side.

(the café)

The next time she spotted Tom, though, on Saturday afternoon, she headed straight for him. He was in the same café on the corner, sitting at a table near the window. This time he was alone, with a book open on the table in front of him, although he was staring out onto the sidewalk and caught Nicole's glance immediately. Nicole didn't hesitate: she entered the café and threaded her way through the tables until she reached him.

"Excuse me," Nicole began.

Tom stood up quickly, a welcoming smile on his face, and began to pull out a chair so she could join him.

"Could I ask you for a favor?" Nicole asked, not sitting down. She wanted to borrow a quarter, she said. Sure, Tom agreed, and reached into his pocket to find one for her. He held the quarter out to Nicole, but she didn't take it.

"Actually, what I need is," she began, sounding slightly embarrassed, "for you to take the quarter and put it in the pay phone outside and dial a number for me. Okay?"

Tom was bewildered but followed Nicole out to the pay phone on the corner, dropped the quarter in the slot, and dialed the number she recited to him. He waited just long enough to make sure the phone was ringing, handed the receiver to Nicole, and then stepped a discreet distance away.

"I'm sorry, I can't make it," he heard Nicole say in a low voice. She sounded edgy. "Something's come up. It can't be helped. . . ." There was a pause, and then she raised her voice. "I said I'm sorry." She hung up the phone and rejoined Tom, who hadn't overheard a thing, of course. Nicole gave him a bright smile.

"I had to cancel an appointment with my hairdresser," she announced. "But now I could really use a glass of wine."

"My pleasure," Tom answered, steering her back into the café and toward his table.

When their drinks came, Nicole raised her glass to Tom. "Cheers. *L'chayim,*" she said jauntily. She was in a very good mood, effervescent. "You've just become my *shabbos goy.*"

She laughed at the expression on Tom's face.

"Today is the Jewish sabbath—*shabbos,*" Nicole explained. "Or *shabbat.* You just did something for me that I'm forbidden to do on shabbat."

"I may have heard of it," Tom said dryly. "But go on. What's the big deal?"

Nicole started from scratch. "I'm an observant Jew. *Frum,* we call it—pious. Law-abiding. You might call it my cult." She sounded pleased with herself, teasing Tom; she knew that even if he had been waiting for this encounter, he hadn't bargained for it to happen in quite this way. "I keep the sabbath; I *guard* it, is what you say in Hebrew. That's why you had to put a quarter in the phone for me. I don't handle money on the sabbath." Nicole reached into the pockets of her jacket as if to shake them out. "See?" she asked. "Empty. I'm not carrying a cent."

"Why not?" Tom asked.

Nicole hesitated. "I don't really know," she confessed after a moment's thought. "We just don't, that's all. No commercial transactions, I guess, but I don't know exactly why. Actually, there are a lot of things forbidden on the sabbath. You can't work. Or ride in a car. Or—"

"Or use the phone?" Tom interrupted. "I'm beginning to get the drift."

Nicole grinned. "It was just for a second."

"In for a penny, in for a pound," Tom was quick to point out, enjoying himself. He leaned forward and touched Nicole's hand for a second. "That's what we say in *my* cult. I'm what you might call an observant Christian."

Nicole was pleased to hear it.

"We observant Christians," he continued, "are sometimes a bit harsh on hypocrites. In fact, we have several modest attacks on them in our literature. They're called *gospels*, which means good news, although, to be honest, the news is almost all bad."

"It always is," Nicole agreed.

Tom nodded. "By the way," he continued, "how were you planning to pay your hairdresser?"

Nicole was not at all nonplussed. "What you're really asking," she said soberly, "is how I can justify not carrying money on the sabbath and still telephone the man I am having an affair with." Before Tom could interrupt, before he could sidestep her with some polite hypocrisy of his own, Nicole rushed ahead. "The answer is that I decided at the last minute I didn't want to see him."

"And if you hadn't decided that you didn't want to see him?"

"Hmmm," said Nicole. "I can tell you think there's something inconsistent in my position."

"A shade."

Nicole took a deep breath. "All right," she said. "I'm married, but . . . my husband and I don't get along. We probably should get divorced, but we don't seem to be able to untangle ourselves. Besides . . . we have two kids . . . so I lead a very complicated life. I go to *shul*—synagogue, that is—every Saturday, and I have a lover. I keep kosher—"

"Keep kosher?" asked Tom, following closely.

"Observe the Jewish dietary laws—*kashrut*. You don't mix milk and meat. But I often see the man you overheard me talking to, and we make love. If you want a justification, I can't—I won't—give it to you."

Nicole downed the rest of her wine in one gulp. Tom did the same. There was a long silence. Nicole was the first to break it, by beginning to stand up. She suddenly realized that she had overextended herself. "Thank you so much for the wine," she said. "Now, if you'll excuse me—"

Tom jumped to his feet, reached into his pocket, and dropped several bills on the table, swiftly, all in one motion, and then propelled Nicole through the crowded café and back onto the street. "I'm walking you home," he announced.

"Uh, no," Nicole began, "I'm not ready to—"

"Neither am I," agreed Tom. "So, where do you want to go? We'll walk there. I wouldn't dream of taking a cab. I don't know if you realize this, but it's the Jewish sabbath."

Nicole giggled. "I was going to my hairdresser," she said, pointing.

"Didn't you just blow him off?" Tom asked wryly. When Nicole had no answer, he took her arm and led her down the street.

(Broadway)

Five blocks later, Tom had told Nicole his life story or, at least, the skeleton of it. That he grew up in the South, where his father owned the largest drugstore in town—where a man had been murdered, out of nowhere, it seemed, right before Tom's eyes. Tom had stopped in one day after school, ostensibly to say hello to his daddy but really to stand at the magazine rack to read the latest issue of *The New Yorker*. Sometimes he stole a copy, from his own father, hiding it under his shirt and spiriting it home. Even then—Tom smiled at the memory—he'd been plotting to escape and head up to New York. A well-dressed man was paying for something at the counter when all of a sudden a shot rang out. The man swayed for a second and then slumped onto the floor, his wallet beside him and enough bills on the floor to pay for every magazine on the shelf. Tom had been hustled out of the pharmacy pretty fast. The worst part, as far as Tom was concerned, was that he, too, had dropped to the floor at the sound of the shot—in fact, he thought for a second that maybe he had been shot for stealing *New Yorker*s. After all, they fed his guilty fantasies about leaving forever to become an artist or, better yet, a cartoonist, drawing clever scenes that no one back home could possibly understand. From that day on, his father always carried a small pistol in an ankle holster. The silver-tipped cane had been his father's, too. It was hollow, said Tom, demonstrating for Nicole by unscrewing the tip. He had always suspected his father kept contraband in it—money, perhaps, for a quick getaway, or a knife. It's a dangerous business, ordinary life.

Tom's mother was the daughter of missionaries; she saw to it that Tom went to Bible school every Wednesday evening and before church on Sunday mornings. Yes, they bowed their heads and said grace before every meal, and yes, when he was eleven Tom was not only stealing *New Yorker*s but had accepted Jesus Christ as his personal Lord and Savior and had been baptized, on Pentecost, in a large vat of water that he waded into, in his white shirt and underpants, while the pastor stood over him and prayed.

Tom kept his eyes on Nicole while he told her of his baptism—it was one thing, he knew, to confess to his early life of crime but quite another to retrieve for her that first moment of divine grace and comprehension of the Kingdom of Heaven. But Nicole looked beguiled and even touched, so Tom took a deep breath and continued. His parents had wanted him to go to the University of Virginia and become a minister or, better yet, a lawyer, but he was desperate to become an artist and had fled to New York City, just as he had always planned. To please them, though, he had instead become an architect; it had seemed an appropriate compromise. And he was awfully good at it for a while, as Jules had said. Until things fell apart.

Tom admitted that he didn't have the fortitude of Nicole's tribe, to endure seven lean years. Two or three were quite enough. He needed to redeem himself somehow; he needed to put his life back in order. When Tom was rueful, he leaned on the cane a bit more, as if he had some distant memory of injury. He had retrieved the cane,

he said, when his father died. It was the only thing he had
wanted.

But suddenly Tom stopped, in the middle of the block.
"I want to show you something," he began, facing a large
building and pointing upward with his cane. "It's something so awful, I've never told anyone about this. Ever."

Nicole looked where Tom was pointing. All she saw
was the gray limestone facade of the kind of apartment
house found all over Manhattan's Upper West Side.

"She used to live there," Tom continued. "The third
floor—those two windows on the left."

Nicole nodded.

"She was an actress, Polish. She spoke almost no
English, but I was wild about her. We played cards all the
time—day and night. Finally—this is the part I haven't
told anyone—she had an abortion. Without telling me.
And then she bolted." Tom looked stricken, angry, as if he
might abruptly start to cry. But he grabbed Nicole's arm
again. "Come on," he said, "let's go."

They walked two more blocks, in silence. This time
Nicole stopped and pointed down the side street. "There,"
she said gently, "in that brownstone. Someone way before
David. We used to play a game he called *third degree*.
He'd make me sit in a chair and shine a light on my face.
Then he'd grill me—you know, *we have ways to make you
talk*. But he never touched me. It got me crazed." Nicole
shook her head at the memory. "I can't believe I did that."

Tom shook his head, too, as if he couldn't believe it,
either. "Someone who would do that," he agreed, "would
do anything."

Nicole laughed. Suddenly the two of them were standing there, on the street corner, doubled over, laughing like maniacs.

Tom straightened up slowly, still laughing, leaning on his cane; he raised his arm and hailed a cab. "Now, I want you to do something for me," he said. "Please." He opened the door of the taxi for Nicole. This time she really demurred.

"I can't," she said, the laughter subsiding. "It really *is* my sabbath, no joke. I don't ride on the—"

"You don't use telephones, either. You told me that very clearly," Tom answered, taking her by the arm. "Come on, get in."

Nicole slid into the taxi with Tom next to her, and he pulled the door closed.

(the taxi)

Make a right," he instructed the driver, "and then a left on Riverside Drive. Left again on Eighty-sixth. Left again on Broadway."

Nicole was taken aback. It was bad enough to jump into a cab with Tom in violation of the sabbath. Even worse—or was it better?—what Tom had proposed to the driver was not a route to a destination, but merely a circle leading back to the café where they had started. She wanted to remonstrate with him, or at least to question him, but after giving his instructions, he had thrown himself against the seat, head back, eyes closed, as if he were fast asleep. By this time the driver was turning onto Riverside Drive, heading south.

Nicole waited for a moment, studying Tom. Out the window, Riverside Drive was as busy as it was every Saturday afternoon, with people pushing strollers, riding bicycles, lovers walking arm in arm, children on slides and swings at the playgrounds that occurred about every two blocks. She noticed uneasily that several couples and families were taking the traditional shabbat afternoon stroll: they were clearly identifiable by their formal clothes, the men in dark suits and wearing hats or yarmulkes, the women and children dressed up, too; but what really gave them away was that no one carried anything. Nicole herself, as she had told Tom, was carrying no money and would not have been able to pay for the cab. What had started out as a flirtatious joke had left her—at least for the moment—financially dependent on Tom. He was still immobile, as if overcome with exhaustion.

Reaching out, he reached out and took her hand, his eyes still closed. He squeezed it hard. "I can't let you go," he whispered so quietly that Nicole could hardly hear him. She leaned closer and waited, hoping he would say something more, but he was silent; he seemed anguished, still urgently holding on to her hand, his eyes tightly shut. He was as rigidly unmoving as if he were paralyzed. Nicole thought that now she knew what it would be like to see someone in a straitjacket. Someone violent, in pain, deliberately restrained. "My love," she whispered.

Suddenly he sat upright, pulling Nicole to him and crushing her against his chest. "I'm blasted, can't you see?" he said hoarsely, holding her so tightly that she could barely breathe. Pressed against him, she couldn't see his face, but she could feel the quickness of his breathing, the tension in his body. He was rigid, very warm, his arms encircling her so that she could hardly move. He held her head to his chest, stroking her hair as if he were consoling her. As if he would like to care for her, love her, if only he could.

"Stop here," Tom commanded abruptly; the taxi came to a quick halt. Already they were back on Broadway, across the street from the café they had left not even an hour before. Tom grabbed a bill from his pocket, thrust it at the driver, and shoved open the door without waiting for his change. Nicole stumbled out after him, into the broad daylight of shabbat afternoon, as if released from a cave.

(outside, on the street)

Nearby on the sidewalk, a man was watching them as they spilled out of the cab, unsettled by how precipitous their ride had been and how much they had already revealed to each other. Each of them had knowingly handed the other a loaded gun. Nicole suddenly gave Tom a kiss on the cheek and swiftly disappeared into the crowd, heading for home.

As Tom walked away, forgetting to lean on his cane,

Jules moved from the building that had half hidden him and stepped into Tom's path.

Tom was startled. "Jules!" he exclaimed.

"I see you've been with our friend," Jules said casually. "You wouldn't know the first thing about this, but she's religious. Nicole doesn't ride on the sabbath."

"Really!" said Tom dryly. "How interesting. But now I see what you people mean by observant."

"Tom," countered Jules, "you are an evil influence."

(Sebastian's)

Nicole was not at all surprised when, two days later, just as she was gathering her books to go home, Tom turned up at the door to her office and asked her to have dinner with him. It didn't even cross her mind that they had known each other barely a week and already Tom knew exactly where to locate her. Nicole herself had done almost nothing else since alighting from the taxi on shabbat but think about him constantly. She was appalled at herself for so quickly and easily violating the sabbath, but she knew also that Tom, in his way, had reciprocated—he, too, had given something up to her, as an offering, a gift. So whenever she had a moment of quietude, Tom would surge into view; she would lose herself in talking to him, telling him stories, explaining things, until some ordinary event interrupted her, wrenching her back to her daily

tasks. He was with her as she cared for her children, pre-
pared her classes, talked on the phone, went to the grocery
store. Sometimes she simply stopped what she was doing
to lean against a wall and think of him. Even though she
writhed inwardly at the memory, she had already told
him, without guile and in total honesty, everything he had
asked about her, no matter how damaging; now she
wanted to tell him more, tell him everything. And to
search him out, too; *to make him talk,* to shine a spotlight
on him until he held nothing back. So dinner would be
perfect—indeed, exactly what she most wanted. Without
Jules, Tom said, and they would have to move quickly so
as not to be intercepted. Nicole hesitated. She would have
to telephone home and concoct something to spring herself for the evening.

She could call from the restaurant, Tom pointed out;
he wanted to get going. He meant it, too: he put his hand
on the small of her back and practically pushed her out
the building, propelling her down the path of the campus
to the street. Broadway was at its busiest, full of rush-hour
traffic; cars were whizzing by with barely a break. They
paused a moment at the curb, and then, suddenly, seeing
an opening, Tom grabbed Nicole by the hand and yanked
at her as if he were pulling a kite.

"Run!" he commanded, holding on to Nicole and
dashing out into the traffic. "Run like hell!" They flew
and dodged their way at breakneck speed through the on-
rush of cars, Tom brandishing his walking stick aloft.
Somehow they landed safely on the other side of the highway, gasping for breath and laughing hilariously. Tom
flagged down a cab. He knew of a place, he said, looking

very pleased with himself, not a great place but a little restaurant he liked and wanted Nicole to see. Jump in.

Twenty minutes later they were at Sebastian's, two glasses of white wine in front of them and hovering waiters who seemed to know Tom and be happy to see him. But Sebastian's was hardly the modest place Tom had advertised. Just a few steps from Fifth Avenue, Sebastian's was actually a large and distinctly elegant restaurant in a whitened, airy, Santa Monica sort of way, as if the winds from the Pacific Ocean were breezing in, lightening the white linen, the crystal wineglasses, and the heavy silverware. Everything seemed bleached and silvery except for the polished mahogany curved bar and the many abstract expressionist paintings hung carefully on the white walls. Almost every table in the restaurant was full when Nicole and Tom blew in without a reservation and checked their coats, but still the maître d' had greeted Tom warmly and said that his old table was ready for him. "Table fifteen," he murmured to the waiter who came to escort Nicole and Tom to the back corner of the restaurant, where a verdant city garden was still visible through the windows as the night air darkened.

Nicole took a quick glance at the menu, and although she was shocked by the prices, she was pleased to see that she could easily order some fresh fish and a green salad and still keep within the boundaries of *kashrut*. She suddenly felt terribly underdressed, though, in what she thought of as her "school clothes," when every other woman at Sebastian's seemed to be in something shimmering and luxurious, mostly black and modishly nipped in at the waist. Tom, however, seemed to fit right in, sartorially speaking; in fact, Nicole suddenly realized how expensively dressed he was, how his trousers were pleated in exactly the right places and how his silky tweed jacket was perfectly cut and fitted. David dressed lavishly, too, but a little eccentrically, his taste running to schoolboy rep ties set off by monogrammed shirts and sometimes even suspenders, as if he were hoping for a compliment from the headmaster. But at least one of his fashion concerns was to follow the precept in Deuteronomy, "Thou shalt not wear mingled stuff, wool and linen together." This "mingled stuff"—*shaatnez* in Hebrew—was strictly off-limits, prohibited, although no one would ever know about a violation. Nevertheless, David, like other observant Jews, always had the tailor who did his alterations snip off a small piece of fabric to send to the *shaatnez* lab in New Jersey, where the admixture of threads would be tested and rabbinically verified.

In the split second of noticing Tom's clothes and thinking about *shaatnez*, Nicole was suddenly flooded with the memory of other prohibitions: not plowing with an ox and a donkey yoked together, not taking a baby bird from its nest in the presence of its mother, not sowing two kinds of seed in a vineyard. Not layering your seed in the wife of your neighbor or uncovering the nakedness of a woman not your own. *If a man be found lying with the wife of another man, both of them shall die*, remembered Nicole, although in the instant she recalled the text she tried to put it out of her mind. *Ye shall stone them with stones that they die.* She studied the menu assiduously, knowing that Tom might very well embody prohibitions other than the "mingled stuff" of his expensive jacket, forbidden acts whose discovery called for death by stoning. But nothing has happened, she thought. She had merely been noticing Tom's clothes. Yet it was undeniably thrilling—and disquieting—to be sitting at Sebastian's across from the man she thought about constantly and whose very clothes were taboo. Later she would worry about death by stoning.

Before they ordered, Tom reminded Nicole that they had to find a phone. He insisted on accompanying her downstairs where the rest rooms and public telephones were and squeezing himself into the phone booth with her when she made her telephone call to the housekeeper, who would put dinner on the table for the children and wait there until David got home. Nicole was so sorry: she had *totally* forgotten that she had to attend a symposium that night and wouldn't be home until much later. The children shouldn't wait up for her, and David could supervise baths and tuck them in. Jacob was not to watch TV until he finished his homework, *all* his homework.

When they returned to the table, Tom couldn't help remarking that it was the second time he had heard her lie over the telephone. Nicole took a deep breath and knocked back a glass of wine. So did Tom, suddenly shy. There was silence. After all, despite the quarter, despite the taxicab, they hardly knew each other. If you had asked Nicole what Tom liked for breakfast, or whether he had ever been to San Francisco, or what the name of his sister was, or whether he even had a sister, she would not have been able to say.

Tom cleared his throat, he hemmed and hawed, and finally he started a long story about how he had spent the day at a site in upstate New York where he was the consulting architect on some mixed-income housing, a new project, and how it was going to be difficult getting the land use variances from the town council. Mixed-income housing was a far cry from the museums and Malibu "villas" he was used to, he admitted, smiling ruefully but looking dispirited. Nicole herself suddenly felt a little worn out. She apologized for seeming tired and explained that, honestly, she wasn't used to going out much in the middle of the week, that her long days with the kids and housework and what seemed like endless hours of teaching left her pretty exhausted by dinnertime. No, she didn't want to go home; she wanted to be right where she was, but she wouldn't mind another glass of wine. Tom signaled the waiter and confessed that he, too, was not in the best of shape. For reasons he would tell her about soon, visiting this housing site left him feeling anxious and depressed, so all he had wanted to do was get back to the city in the hopes of waylaying Nicole. He had a question, something he had thought of during the taxicab ride; he had been meaning to ask.

Who has hurt you the most? But she couldn't talk about it, not then. So while all she had done was weep for a split second and turn the question back to him, Nicole knew that she would tell him. Eventually, but not now. Because of course she had been hurt—badly, too; people do that to each other, they damage each other, it is inevitable. All it takes is a brutal word from one person to the other, a day or two of angry silence, some almost imperceptible kamikaze act of destruction, and a line is crossed that can never be erased. Like Tom, Nicole had one particular person in mind, someone she had "gotten over," finally. Gotten over to the point where now she wondered what she had ever seen in him, why she had ever felt so obsessed. Eventually she would have to tell Tom her own story; she would even want to tell him about it, to give him the story as a gift.

Her story was not as dramatic as Tom's. She hadn't walked the streets as Tom had. She hadn't threatened to kill herself. She had just simply gone on with her life, worked at her job, tended her children, whom she loved beyond belief. Everything else got shelved. But she had kept within herself the knowledge that when two people are in love, one of them will fall out of love first. Who had hurt her the most was not the sort of question David would ever have asked her. In fact, no one would have asked her that question. Until Tom.

(Sebastian's)

Nicole and Tom seemed to be spending quite a lot of time at Sebastian's, table fifteen. First dinner, and then lunch almost every day that week, and the entire afternoon until the very last minute when Nicole would have to rush off to meet her children after school. No one ever bothered them or suggested that lunch was long over. They could spend hours and hours at their table, almost without moving, telling each other stories about everyone they ever knew, who had bruised them and who had consoled them, whom they had behaved nobly toward or despicably, what Nicole had lectured upon in her Bible class that morning, what book Tom was reading, and the funny thing that just happened on the way over. Tom said that he was now including her in his nightly "God bless" catalog—he had short-listed her, she would be glad to know—and Nicole retorted that she never mentioned him at all to God, that *her* tradition obliged her to pray for much weightier things like the restoration of ancient sacrifice, may it come speedily, in our days. Tom confessed that he kept a pair of spyglasses at his drawing board so he could peer at women undressing in the fashion showroom across the way. Nicole revealed her embarrassing fantasy that a stranger was watching her from a doorway while she lay naked on a bed, telling her, *either you do it yourself or I'll do it for you,* and Tom wanted to know if she really believed in love at first sight or wasn't it more likely that you fall in love because somehow you know that the other person is already in love with you?

In the midst of one of these conversations, when it seemed that the world could end without their paying the least attention, Tom suddenly looked up and bolted from his seat. By the time Nicole had swiveled around to see where he was going, Tom was locked in embrace with another woman. Nicole watched, mesmerized, as Tom covered her with hugs and kisses. She couldn't tell what they were saying, but she could hear muffled bursts of affection and laughter as Tom walked the woman to the door, all the while hugging her and smiling delightedly.

It dawned on Nicole, who couldn't take her eyes from this performance, that he was not so much accompanying the woman to the door as hustling her out, expertly screening each woman from view of the other. Nevertheless, Nicole managed to note that the stranger was blond, artificially tanned, and rail thin, with the tight skin and slanted eyes of someone who has treated herself to face lifts.

"Your wife?" Nicole demanded caustically when Tom sauntered back to the table. "Or just some platinum blonde wondering if you know a good plastic surgeon?"

Tom didn't look the least sheepish; in fact, Nicole's question obviously amused him. It was no one, he said, smiling broadly, just an old friend of his wife's who caught him off guard. Sorry; it was terribly bad manners, he knew.

"Old friend!" Nicole exploded. "You were crawling all over her!"

Tom burst out laughing. "Tell you what—" he began, signaling the waiter and making handwriting gestures in the air so that the waiter would bring the bill. He signed without even paying attention to the amount he was writing off, then stood up, gesturing for Nicole to come with him and putting his hand under her elbow to practically yank her out of her chair.

Once out on the sidewalk he propelled her into the nearest doorway. She stiffened, abashed at having given herself away in an outburst of fury and jealousy. She should never have watched them, she thought, she should have turned aside nonchalantly. But she couldn't help it, and now she really did feel naked.

Tom put his arms around Nicole, who was doing her best to remain guarded and aloof. He looked happy, delighted. "I'll give up the platinum blonde—I'll give up the dark one," he was murmuring, pulling her closer to him, wrapping his arms more tightly around her. "They're history, I promise," he continued, nuzzling her with such intensity that Nicole had to relent; she couldn't help it—she softened, feeling his body against hers. When he had held her that first time in the taxicab, he had been urgent and tense, as if reaching for her out of his private desperation; now his body felt different, relaxed and sensual. He wanted her and was enjoying himself. She didn't say a word; suddenly she could hardly breathe.

"But if you want to know what crawling all over someone is like. . . ," he whispered, running his hands over her shoulders, back, sides, buttocks, touching her everywhere, through her clothes and beneath them, wherever he could reach. Nicole's eyes closed; she felt the lassitude that is something like sleep, a fullness welling up and overcoming her, deep and pleasurable. She still hardly knew this man, yet she had known from the first moment that they would touch each other, that he would uncover himself completely to her and she to him. He cupped her face with both hands, waiting for her to look at him, asking without words if she were his, listening for her calm and wordless assent. Then he found the words: *My heart swerved.*

For a moment he hesitated. But when they kissed, it

was for a long time. As if there were time. In broad daylight, in the midst of passersby and cars and all the humdrum traffic of the city, none of which made the slightest difference; it could have been the blackest night in the farthest desert for all they knew or cared. Not a sound reached them except their own breathing.

I would be your sister and brother, all your cousins, your mother and father. I would kiss you on the mouth and make you promise not to tell, I would go with you to the hiding places in the tall grasses and make you come into my hand. I would say grace with you before meals with our heads bent, and every night at bedtime I would bring you cookies and milk and tuck you in. I would let you play hooky from school and take you to movies that you're too young to understand. I would find the dirty magazines you hid under the mattress. I would give you baths and soap you everywhere. . . .

Later, when we are alone, I will undress you, slowly, piece by piece, touching your body, every part. I will kiss your neck where the blood pulses, I will lick it with my tongue. I will touch your nipples lightly, with my fingertip, my tongue, until you harden and rise, lifting yourself toward me, asking me with your body to touch you more, further, harder. I will clasp you with my knees and rise above you; you will come with me. Wherever I am you will come with me.

(Sebastian's)

The next day at Sebastian's, Nicole and Tom first greeted each other with a firm handshake, then locked themselves for a second into an enormous embrace, disentangling only to slide awkwardly onto their chairs as if they had just met. After filling each other in on the events of the past twenty hours since they had parted, Nicole was full of questions; there was so much she still didn't know. She set down her wineglass with a deliberate air and inquired about the motorcycle. She was sure she had heard Jules say something about Tom's wife being on it.

"It was a car," Tom said grimly. "It was bad enough with a car."

Nicole waited to hear more, but Tom was silent. He tried to talk once or twice, but whatever he was saying quickly became garbled, so he threw up his hands and gave up.

What he finally blurted out was not at all what Nicole expected.

"I've always wanted to be a saint," Tom suddenly confessed, shifting on his chair so that he would not have to look directly at Nicole. Well, if not a saint, a wholly good man, he explained earnestly, facing her again, talking to her urgently. Maybe they're the same, but in any case that had always been his true goal, sainthood. Tom fully expected an afterlife in the company of angels, singing all the hymns from his childhood. He began to laugh at himself, but he was also totally serious.

Nicole was a bit taken aback: she'd never met an incipient saint before, a saint in the making, as it were. Certainly not one who was married, one who devoured other women in restaurants and doorways. "What does one have to do to get canonized?" she asked, intrigued. What did Tom really mean? Was it that vat of water, long ago, that he had marched into in his pure underclothes that had steered him toward the angels? And what *was* sainthood, anyway?

Well, he was not quite sure what he meant, but he supposed that a saint loves his neighbor as himself, turns the other cheek. . . . What he *really* meant, Tom finally decided, warming to the idea, was that he aspired to be benign and compassionate, always to consider the needs and values of the other person before his own, to forgive seventy times seven and more.

"Ever since I was a little kid," he said, "I've tried to be good, to go after some version of sainthood, though I know how ridiculous I sound and how, well, impossible it might be . . . but still, there you are." Tom grinned and shook his head. "I know, I know," he acknowledged, "this is even worse than everything you already know about me." He wouldn't blame Nicole in the least if her eyes glazed over, if she were sorry she ever met him. Who would ever want to have lunch with a saint?

Did wanting to be a saint, Nicole asked, mean that he was never supposed to get angry? Tom thought probably it meant that, too, not to experience anger, certainly not at those you love. Nicole was even more mystified: she got angry *primarily* at those she loved.

True, even Jesus got angry, Tom acknowledged, especially at his own family. So, yes, of course, he got angry—enraged sometimes—but he was always ashamed afterward and would try to make amends by acquiescing to the other person, by trying to find ways to be forgiven. Whoever said sainthood was easy? It was a discipline, he was beginning to understand, a set of boundaries and limits, and even if his life wasn't always in sync with it . . . Tom's voice trailed off.

"What about marriage?" Nicole demanded. "Speaking of limits."

Tom flushed and drew back. Instead of answering, he called for the check and signed for it with his credit card, adding an outrageously large tip and barely glancing at the tally. Once outside, they walked a block or two in silence, not touching each other, each of them lost in thought. Suddenly Tom stopped and stood still, facing her. Nicole looked grave; she was still waiting for an answer.

"Are you a good liar?" Tom inquired instead, leaning on his cane. Nicole considered the question.

Just that day she had pleaded a late afternoon meeting to another Thackeray mother, who had agreed to take over car pool so she could be here with Tom and not be forced to rush off. But no, she said finally. She probably wasn't at all a good liar. "Are you?" she asked.

"Oh, yes," Tom replied, looking uncomfortable but coming clean. "Very good. Far too good, I would say."

Nicole asked what he lied about.

Tom took a deep breath and glanced off into space, avoiding Nicole's eyes. "Everything," he said finally as if he could barely get the word out. "Everything I've said and done—my sainthood, my clothes, even the way I pay the check—it's all been to impress you. They aren't lies exactly, but I'm desperate to show off for you." In an undertone, sounding strangled, he admitted that his marriage, too, even his marriage, was a lie. He himself had blown it up, to his great shame and discredit; it was over. He had to tell her, he said, staring off into the distance. But he would say it only once and then he could never say it again. He still wouldn't meet Nicole's gaze. It suddenly occurred to Nicole that he was afraid of her: he had told her too much; he had given up too much, too readily. His admissions, his confessions, even his lies, had given her tremendous power over him. She knew suddenly that at any moment she could shred him, as he too could pulverize her; each had the power to make the other feel stupidly vulnerable and forever sorry. His confession, wrenched out of him, let her know how afraid he was of how much he needed her, afraid of what he might do to keep her.

"It's painful to be a saint, isn't it," she said, trying to console him, touching him gently. "It makes you dangerous, doesn't it," she continued in a murmur. Tom could only nod, as if confronting some deep and private anguish. Yet nothing he said surprised Nicole in the least; she had known it all from the beginning, from the way he joked and then leaned on his silver-tipped cane as if wounded by his own thoughts, from the way he insisted on castigating himself, calibrating his disclosures to her pleasure. She began to kiss him, trying to soothe him, see-

ing how humiliating it was for him to cleave to his hope
of sainthood while ordinary life betrayed him over and
over.

But he wouldn't be consoled; he could still hardly meet
her gaze. So she took his hand, put his finger into her
mouth, and began to bite down, gently at first, and then
harder and harder, until he cried out and wrenched it
away from her. Her eyes felt heavy; she felt deep and
sleepy and warm, as if he were inside her, everywhere. But
it wasn't enough. Wordlessly Tom offered her his hand
again; he closed his eyes, waiting for what she would do.
Again she bit him, in the same place, gently and then less
gently and then to hurt him, to rouse him, to bring him
back to her so that he would never leave. This time he allowed it, steadied himself for it, although he drew in his
breath sharply as she bit down. When she released him, he
pressed his finger to his own mouth, touching the mark
she had inflicted, as if instead of hurting him she had as-
suaged his pain.

Then he let himself be held and embraced, still anguished, but kissing her back hungrily. She kissed him
deeply, not letting him go. She consoled him with the
depth of her kiss and the softness of her body, showing
him that she would love him and not withhold herself. She
needed him, too, no matter how shattering they would be
for each other, no matter the price. She was as abject as
he; her need was as powerful as his; she was capable of
anything. But she would never leave him: she knew beyond question that she was deeply and forever tied to this
man who was constantly dying and being reborn, right
before her eyes.

(the playground)

Who gave you the fuck-me bracelet?" Jules asked, pointing down at Nicole's ankle. He and Nicole were at the playground with their children in the midst of a small crowd of other parents and children, children on swings and slides, children climbing on bars or careening from one end of the playground to the other, letting off steam after a long day at school. Nicole shaded her eyes, watching Jake as he maneuvered himself around on his first pair of Rollerblades.

"Funny you should notice," she said. "I've worn it for two years."

"I didn't," Jules pointed out. "It was Tom."

"Who?"

"Don't be such a wiseass," Jules retorted. "I know there's something going on. You practically just met and you've been spotted all over town."

"Jake!" Nicole called out. "Get down off that!" She turned to Jules. "He thinks he can do anything, he thinks he's infallible. Did you see how he tried jumping off that ramp?" She waved her arms at her son as if to say, No, stay off that ramp. Be careful.

"That rock star in your biblical lit? The three-earring guy with the handcuffs dangling from his belt?"

"I've been spotted with him?" laughed Nicole. "Great!"

"You know what I'm talking about," Jules persisted, unhinging his small son from his waist and promising to watch him go all the way across the monkey bars, but in a minute, just a minute. "Some guy gave you an ankle bracelet. And now you're hanging out with Tom. I'd be more careful if I were you. You tend to go too far."

Nicole was waving her arms again, signaling to Jake to stop whatever it was he was doing and do something else, something safer, more prudent. Slow down, she was muttering under her breath as if Jake could hear. She and Jules wandered over to the jungle gym, where Jules's son was playing tag with a bunch of other kids. Jules was right: she tended to go too far.

"So where do you guys go?" Jules tried again, making a face as Sam landed on his shoulders for a second and then kicked off in hot pursuit of someone else.

"Oh, the usual drug dens and S and M clubs," Nicole replied airily.

"*You and Tom,*" Jules spelled out. "What are you two up to?"

"Nothing. We just go to a restaurant."

"Yeah? Which one?"

"I'm sure you never heard of it. It's down the street from Tom's office, in midtown. It's called Sebastian's." What Nicole needed was not to chatter about Tom, burbling and humming his name in sickeningly besotted fashion, but to evoke and remember him, to blot out the world and concentrate on him: the memory of his taste and smell and warmth instantly made her dizzy. But instead she talked about Sebastian's. "It's sort of off-the-charts elegant, dreadfully expensive, but Tom says it's a Mafia place. He says the waiters are armed, and—"

"Sebastian's!" Jules interrupted. "Oh, no, not Sebastian's. You actually fell for that line about shootouts? Sebastian's," Jules said condescendingly, "is two blocks from what used to be a notorious clubhouse, so everyone throws around that stuff about the waiters. It's pretentious. Overpriced. But who the hell cares about Sebastian's? I didn't mean what restaurant do you fucking eat in. I meant, *where do you go?*"

"We go to Sebastian's," Nicole answered coldly. "We have lunch."

"Lunch? Lunch? You're only having lunch? You expect me to believe that?" Jules was so indignant that Nicole's eyes widened in amusement.

"Besides," Jules continued, "I can't believe you'd let that thug in your Bible class rope you in with an ankle bracelet. I didn't think you were so tacky."

(Sebastian's)

The waiters were beginning to smile at Tom and Nicole when they walked in and to escort them right to their table, knowing that they would be sitting there all afternoon—they had been doing it every day that week and most of the week before. They would sit down, someone would put two glasses of Tom's special chardonnay in front of them, but Nicole and Tom would hardly even look up. Then, a while later, someone else would materialize from somewhere and say cheerfully, "The usual?" Tom and Nicole would both nod, and that would be that.

They were there again, on Friday afternoon, almost hidden at the far end of Sebastian's. Table fifteen. It was a small rectangular table set simply with its usual white linen tablecloth, heavy silver, and two glasses apiece for wine and mineral water. There was a vase of fresh flowers, but Tom and Nicole had pushed it aside, so that if they wanted to, they could lean across the table and touch each other, signaling, as if no one else were within yards of them. To anyone watching, it would be clear that they were not in this restaurant to eat, even though there was food in front of them. Sometimes one of them would take a bite of something, automatically, without thinking. Or a waiter would come to refill their glasses, but without saying a word to either of them. Even when Nicole and Tom were silent, it would have been almost impossible to interrupt them, so tightly did they establish that invisible wall people can erect when they don't wish to be disturbed. Around them was the usual lunch crowd, a lot of chatter and high spirits, deals done and undone, notches made in the social stock market. None of it touched them in the least.

Beside the food and the wine, there were two books on the table. One was large and militantly serious—a collection of commentaries, ancient and modern, on Leviticus. The other book was somewhat different. It was a small paperback with a garish cover, called *Who? Whom?*— pornography of the seediest sort. It was the kind of book one would pay for quickly and slip away with, to read in private. Apparently Nicole and Tom had brought each other gifts, although *Who? Whom?* was difficult to figure out.

There was a long stretch of silence.

Nicole was the first to break it. "Would you plow with an ox and a donkey yoked together?" she asked. Would he uncover her nakedness, layer his seed where it is prohibited, risk death by stoning? She already knew the answer.

Yes, Tom answered, he would. He didn't even hesitate.

Something was about to shift; they both felt it. Nicole was suddenly consumed with terror—or was it joy? "I'm afraid," she confessed for the first time, knowing that Tom understood. She was more than afraid; she felt shattered. Tom acknowledged that he was afraid, too, and then both of them said that they were deeply, uncontrollably happy.

More silence.

Tom picked up the volume on Leviticus and leafed through it for a moment as if he were seeking something he wanted to discuss with Nicole. Then, leaning forward, he asked, "Nicole? What is it that you really want of me?"

Nicole reached into her handbag. Without a word she rummaged around and then tossed a set of keys across the table to Tom. She would be there tomorrow afternoon, she told him. Around one o'clock. On shabbat.

(Part 2)

(the apartment)

Nicole arrived first. For a moment she thought he wouldn't come, and she was sickened. But then she heard his key as he fumbled for the first time with the lock. He stepped into the foyer, quietly closing the door behind him; after a quick nod at Nicole, he turned around and decisively bolted the door again. But he hardly looked debonair; he seemed stricken, locking the two of them into the apartment and pocketing his keys. He was carrying a shopping bag—lunch, he explained shyly, proffering it, and a bottle of wine, because he knew Nicole wouldn't be carrying anything on the sabbath. Kosher lunch, he said with a smile, but he looked uncomfortable. Consecration wine. It should be the most ordinary thing in the world for a man to visit a friend in an apartment at lunchtime, bringing food, but they both knew that ordinary life, for each of them, had sheered off into mystery some time ago. Their endless hours of talk at Sebastian's, their adhesion to religious obligation and observance, Tom's sainthood and Nicole's piety—all of that had brought them right here, face-to-face and finally alone, in someone else's empty apartment.

In the future, there would come wreckage, unchartable but sure: they would be stoned to death, they would stone each other to death. But what of it? Right now, there was only exhilaration, exultant happiness, and the fear that comes from locking the door behind you. Nicole suddenly couldn't imagine what she was doing, locked in an apartment with a total stranger.

Tom put down his shopping bag. "Show me around," he suggested. Nicole gestured toward the living room; she felt light-headed, helpless. They were both stalling for time.

She stayed by the door, watching Tom as he went slowly from room to room, investigating; she could hear him opening closet doors, the medicine chest in the bathroom, the kitchen cabinets. There was nothing there. As Tom realized that each room was truly empty—not a stick of furniture in the entire place, not a piece—he began to look more relaxed. Soon he was trailing his fingers along the empty walls as if he couldn't believe his good fortune and the emptiness of the space.

They grinned at each other, enjoying themselves, savoring the delay. "Who else have you brought here?" Tom demanded.

"No one," Nicole answered truthfully. "I came here for the first time two days ago. That's how I knew we needed this—" She reached into the pocket of her jacket and pulled out a corkscrew.

In a second the corkscrew was in Tom's pocket and Nicole was pressed to the wall, Tom devouring her, pulling off her jacket, unbuttoning and yanking at her clothes, kissing her mouth, her cheeks, her hair, her neck, while Nicole somehow got her arms free and around Tom, holding him as tightly as she could.

"You'll have to cancel your three o'clock—cancel your five o'clock," Tom ordered, his voice laughing and growling at the same time, shoving his hands under her clothes, one hand on the small of her back, the other beginning to explore her buttocks. His breath was coming quickly.

Nicole nodded her assent, kissing him back, quickening with hunger and warmth, urging him with her body to press against her harder, to take what he had come to the apartment to claim. She promised brokenly, barely able to speak, to give everyone up; she would never see anyone again, anyone, except for him. Soon she would give herself up, too; she would have to; she would give up completely and slide down the wall to the floor.

(the apartment)

Their ritual was to arrive and leave separately, never together. Even if they had been together—having lunch, say, at Sebastian's—they still went separately to the apartment. So although Sebastian's felt illicit to her, clandestine and private even when every other table was filled with people, the apartment was not only clandestine, it was another world altogether. Turning her key in the door made her feel like Persephone, entering her Underworld, doomed. But also expectant, and full of joy. She simply never knew what would happen there. It was an underworld of total mystery and complete familiarity. What could be more ordinary than an empty apartment?

Sometimes Nicole would deliberately arrive much earlier than Tom, to wait there for him. She liked surprising him by getting there first, that was true, but beyond that, she would enact little rituals of domesticity. Not to make the apartment feel like home—she had no interest in that—but to experience the limits of its emptiness. She would enter eagerly, check the bathroom, look to see that there was wine and seltzer in the refrigerator, some paper cups, the corkscrew. Other than the few necessities in the bathroom and kitchen, there was nothing at all in the apartment; each room, each closet and kitchen drawer, was completely empty. The long entry hallway, the bedroom and bathroom opening onto it, the tiny, serviceable kitchen, and the living room at the front of the apartment were simply empty spaces, without any furniture whatsoever, not so much as a chair or a rug, but perfect in their hollow emptiness, unfilled and echoing. The living room with its dining area was large with high ceilings, but a perfectly unadorned rectangle of space, as if it had been designed to be as anonymous as possible. At one end of the room was a brick wall with a small raised fireplace and, over the fireplace's wooden mantel, a mirror, by now dusty and clouded, reflecting the vast emptiness of the room. The whole apartment, in fact, was dusty from weeks of being unused, the air stale and stifling. After checking the refrigerator, Nicole would raise the venetian blinds covering the front windows and then shove the windows wide open to let in some fresh air; afterward she would lower and tilt the blinds again, so that no one across the street could see inside. A chandelier hung incongruously over the space where there had once been a dining room table: even in broad daylight Nicole would flick on the chandelier for its pool of light on the parquet floor. The apartment belonged to a friend who had moved away and had taken all her belongings with her. She had asked Nicole to check on it occasionally while she decided whether to sell it or rent it out. So Nicole had access to it, for a while.

When Nicole had passed the keys to Tom across the table at Sebastian's, he hadn't seemed the least startled. "You'll like it," she had assured him, "you really will. It's your sort of place. Utterly empty. Not a shred of furniture."

Tom not only liked it, he was enchanted by it, and so was Nicole. Because it was empty, they claimed it immediately as their own. They simply opened the door on that shabbat afternoon and knew that the apartment was heaven on earth. All they really wanted to do was stock the refrigerator with some wine and then settle down in a place where there was nothing to do but be with each other.

Nicole could tell him things in the apartment she wouldn't tell him anywhere else. Not even at Sebastian's. That she loved him unrestrainedly, or that she was terrified he would find a reason to leave her. One afternoon in the apartment he had told her he was leaving early, to meet his wife at a restaurant to have a drink. His wife seemed to want some kind of reconciliation—it was a gamble, he had mixed feelings about it, but he was going to do it anyway. Nicole went ashen: for a moment she was afraid she would faint, but instead she had ended up sobbing. "*I'm* not in love with anyone else," she had wept.

"Oh, but you are," Tom had replied, "you just don't want to admit it."

"You don't know what you're talking about," Nicole had said, refusing to be consoled. "But you'd better not meet her at Sebastian's," she had added, going from panic to fury in a matter of seconds.

Tom told her that her life was like a cubist painting, the shapes all jagged and askew, that you have to stand back pretty far to see a pattern. And *his* life, Nicole retorted, was like one of those Flemish wedding portraits where everything seems hunky-dory until you notice a mirror reflecting a scene that couldn't possibly be taking place, something logically impossible. The false mirror was an almost hidden sign, a clue saying "This scene is a fake."

When Nicole charged him, when she said that he might very well be a fake, Tom confessed immediately. It was his way to disarm her, by confessing to fraudulence with his makeshift humility. But he did leave early, to have a drink with his wife. Nicole watched him walk out of the empty apartment and thought to herself, Okay, strike one.

He was sunlit, though. Once when he had entered Sebastian's with the sun directly behind him, streaming through the restaurant's windows, it seemed to Nicole as if he were glowing, enveloped in a shaft of light. Or when he stood in one of the doorways in the apartment, leaning against the frame, gazing at her, sometimes he seemed bathed in sunshine. His hair seemed golden, his jacket golden, everything about him radiantly warmed, as if he had drunk liquid gold for breakfast. She didn't love him because he was golden, though: she loved him because he thought himself a fake.

Sometimes Tom would let himself into the apartment long before Nicole arrived. She would find the door still locked and think she was the first to arrive when really Tom was there waiting for her the whole time. She would walk down the entry hallway and suddenly come across him, sitting on the floor in the empty living room, his back propped against the wall. He would be reading, or drawing, as if he'd been there a long time waiting for her to arrive. It was a slight shock to her, to come across him that way, when she had thought she was entirely alone. Of course he had heard her key in the lock and her footsteps echoing in the hall. When he did that, when he silently waited there for her, catching her off guard, Nicole would feel a tremor of alarm.

If he caught a whiff in the air that she was vulnerable, he would exact more from her. At times like that, he wanted her to undress, to strip for him. He wanted to lounge against the doorjamb and have her stand in the center of the room to take off her clothes. All he wanted to do was just look at her, naked.

What unnerved her even more, though, was that sometimes when they were sitting together on the floor, quietly and companionably talking, he might suddenly tell her to stand up and go to the center of the room. I want you to stand in the middle of the room, he would say, and take off your clothes. All of them. Nicole would take a deep breath and slowly get up, as if she were going to the guillotine. For Tom, because she loved him and he loved her, unquestioningly, she would stand quietly in the center of the empty room and undress. When she was completely naked, he would point to the opposite wall and tell her to walk over there and stand still. *I want you to face the wall,* he would say. He always said please. *Please stand over there, against the wall,* he would say. *Please turn around and face the wall.* The reason it unnerved her so much was that she never quite knew what was coming. After all, she couldn't see him. She was simply supposed to face the wall, naked. Not to touch it, not to lean against it, but just to face it.

Of course she could have refused, but she never did. It never even crossed her mind as a possibility.

Instead she felt utterly stripped, undressed and obedient. *Don't move,* Tom would say, *please stand still. I am just looking at you.* Nicole would stand there, immobile, waiting for something to happen. It terrified her, that waiting. It would terrify her to be so naked, even though she had taken her clothes off as if undressing for a man in an empty apartment were the most natural thing in the world. Nor was it the first time she had taken off her clothes for a man, that went without saying. But when he told her to turn away from him and face the wall, all of her bravado would vanish. Then Tom would walk over to her, slowly, until he was right next to her, his body only a millimeter away. He would not have allowed her to look around anyway, but she didn't need to, she knew how close he was. She could feel him breathing, his voice a deep whisper in her ear. Even then, he didn't touch her. He wouldn't touch her, but leaned close to her, drinking in her embarrassment, her terror, until she was distraught and overcome by the blankness of the wall and the depth of her need to obey him.

But if she needed to obey him, she knew that he needed it, too, maybe even more than she did. He needed her to stand naked against the wall, he needed to show her that she had to do it, unquestioning, simply because he asked her to. Eventually she would force the same obedience upon him. Make him surrender when he least wanted to, when he least thought he could. They never talked about it, but they both knew they had struck a bargain. If she were chained to him, naked and facing a wall, he was chained to her, equally. They knew that his forcing her to the blank wall, while he stood and watched, left him just as stripped and naked as she was.

They both knew, without ever speaking of it, that that was what the empty apartment was for, to act out the terrifying depth of their need for each other. To wind the chain one more time around.

(the apartment)

We're going to take care of this," Nicole announced suddenly to Tom, putting down her glass of wine with a definitive gesture. She was sitting on the floor next to him in the empty living room, her back propped against the blank wall, shoulder to shoulder with Tom. The remains of their lunch were littered around them, a half-empty bottle of wine, the newspaper, Nicole's jacket, folded neatly.

Tom was in a very good mood. Next to him on the floor was his sketchpad, where, waiting for Nicole's entry, he had been drawing plans for an installation of his architectural drawings at a local gallery and for a new museum of contemporary art on Long Island. Nothing definite yet, but perhaps he wasn't such a pariah after all. Too early to tell, but things might be looking up.

"Take care of what?" he asked amiably.

"You," Nicole replied decisively, swinging her body around so that she could face Tom and take him by the shoulders. "And high time, too. . . ," she began, but then she trailed off. There were some things she couldn't say, even to Tom. Instead she regarded him critically. She took the paper cup of wine from his hand and set it carefully on the floor some distance away from them so that it wouldn't spill.

"Stand up," she ordered.

Tom glanced at Nicole warily.

He reached for his paper cup of wine, thought better of it, and withdrew his hand. Still Nicole said nothing. Tom shrugged in resignation. Slowly he got to his feet.

Nicole stood up, too, and kissed him lightly, sweetly, but the kiss was a bit more purposeful than usual, a kiss meant to make him uncomfortable. Then she stepped back a pace, unwound the silk scarf from around her neck, methodically rolled it up again, and placed it carefully over his eyes. He didn't resist.

"Don't move," she said severely, meaning it, a little

menacing. He didn't move a muscle, he barely took a breath, but stood there like a robot while Nicole knotted the scarf at the back of his head. Not to torment him, but to show him, unmistakably, that, just as she had said, it was her turn now.

"There," she said matter-of-factly, checking her work. Tom still didn't move, but stood stock still, blinded, waiting to see what Nicole would do to him next. Even though he was perfectly free to, he didn't lift a hand to remove the scarf, nor did he reach out to touch Nicole. He did as he was told.

"Now—" said Nicole, and didn't finish her sentence. Instead she ran her hands over his face, his neck, his shoulders, down his arms. Then she began kissing him in earnest, her mouth pressed to his and her tongue searching for him, finding him where he was deep and hidden. He shivered slightly and then gave in to her, kissing her back, blindly. When Tom finally couldn't help himself any longer, he tried to put his arms around her, to draw her closer to him, but Nicole pulled away from him. She positioned his arms once again at his sides and held them there for a moment.

"I said, don't move," Nicole warned sternly, and began kissing him again. This time he obeyed.

So Nicole kissed his face, his neck, holding him by the shoulders and then running her hands up and down his sides. Tom shuddered, taking deep breaths, opening and closing his hands as if he wanted to touch Nicole, reach for her, but didn't dare. Slowly, making him feel her movements because he couldn't see her, Nicole removed his tie and began unbuttoning his shirt.

"Are you frightened?" she asked, unbuttoning each button.

"No," Tom whispered. "I trust you."

"Good," said Nicole. She finished unbuttoning his shirt, slid it off, and let it fall to the floor. Tom didn't move. Then she took his hand, pulled up her sweater slightly, and ran his fingers around the inside of the waistband of her skirt. "What do you think I'm wearing?" she asked, replacing his hand at his side.

"I don't know," Tom murmured. "Tell me."

So Nicole told him, while she lightly stroked his chest, his arms, the sides of his body. She told him what she was wearing under her clothes, what color, what fabric, what it felt like against her skin. She told him what she might put on or take off, how she could do it herself or how he could do it for her. She told him what parts of her body were his and what parts were forbidden. She told him what it was like to be alone in the cavernous, blank room with him and what it might be like if someone else, someone unknown, perhaps a woman, entered the room and saw the two of them standing there, Tom blindfolded and half undressed, Nicole caressing him. She ran her fingers over Tom's chest, his ribs, put her mouth to his breast, to his chest, to the nape of his neck, while she went on with her stories in little bursts and murmurs. Soon Nicole was murmuring almost nothing, keeping Tom pressed to her, holding his hands in hers, exploring him with her mouth, flicking him with her tongue, sometimes whispering another fragment of story to him as if she were unscrolling a film. His body was soft, pliable, wonderfully warm and fragrant; he was giving off warmth and sweetness; his body was hers for the asking.

Warm as he was, Tom shivered uncontrollably now and again, his skin lightly shimmering and trembling, but mostly he stood still, as if he were cast in stone. He was trying to remain immobile while his body was moving more and more out of his control, bending and swaying in response to Nicole's touch, her voice, her breath on him, her hands molding his buttocks, his hips, his flesh, wherever he was softened and vulnerable.

"You are beautiful," Nicole whispered, her stories forgotten and thinking only of Tom standing there so obediently, willingly blinded by her scarf, vulnerable, giving himself up. She knew that sometime he would do the same to her, make her give up. He would pin her hands behind her back, bind her wrists with twine or Velcro, leave her helpless. She knew that with her wrists bound, she would become shamefully abject, would beg and plead with him to release her, to make love to her. But that would come later. Now it was her turn. "So good," she continued almost rhapsodically, mesmerized by her power over him. "You *are* mine, aren't you." She leaned down to kiss his belly and started to unhook his belt.

But as Nicole began to slide his trousers down around his hips, Tom suddenly let out an anguished, wordless cry and wrenched himself away from her. Pulling the silk scarf from his eyes, he bolted into the bathroom. By the time Nicole reached him, Tom had hurled himself over the sink as if he were about to throw up. He had opened the tap to a big gush of water and was rapidly splashing water on his face, choking or coughing or sobbing. Nicole grabbed him, circling him with her arms.

"I can't," Tom choked, his whole body heaving while Nicole held on to him. "I can't, I can't. You know I can't."

Slowly he turned off the water and stood up shakily, staring at himself in the bathroom mirror, his face contorted, his eyes blackened and full of pain. Nicole watched him in the mirror, but he wouldn't meet her gaze.

Finally Tom allowed himself to look at Nicole in the mirror and stared at her for a long moment, stony, desperate, gathering himself together to speak.

"Don't ever," he pleaded quietly, "don't ever do that to me again. Ever. Please."

(the apartment)

How can we make love to each other? you want to know in your desperation, your anguish, remembering how you ended up gagging over the sink, trying to drown yourself in floods of water, remembering how, when you finally allowed yourself to look at me, you begged me never to touch you again. It was unbearable, you said, my touch. And then you said you never, ever wanted to see me again. Ever.

You say you are maimed—*spiritually* wounded, you insist, as well as confounded and betrayed by that part of your body that now matters to you most. The first time you allowed yourself to tell me, you cried in a way I had never seen a man cry before: you were lying on the bare floor of the apartment stark naked, but you suddenly cringed when I touched you, and then you doubled up and cried like a child, sobbing and shaken, from some deep, uncontrollable anguish. I didn't even try to touch you then; I just watched, as you have watched me so many times, in unbearable love for you. It is terrible for you to say these things to me, even now when you are finished with crying; you can barely look at me when you talk like this, and your whole body flickers with pain.

But we both somehow knew it before now, even from the very first moment we met; already you knew everything about my body, as I knew everything about yours. Just from looking at each other, feeling the pillows of air as they warmed and cooled in eddies around us. The simple truth is that neither of us has withheld ourselves at all. So I am not surprised that the more completely you are with me, the more totally we belong to each other and consume each other, the less you can make love to me in the way you most want to. Unthinkingly—as you've made love to many others before me. Nor do I care. I've always known that you were blasted. Shattered, you are more mine than if you could saunter away, hale and hearty, swinging your walking stick with its silvery knob. It is not the rich man who enters the Kingdom of Heaven.

However blasted you are, however tethered beyond repair to your failure, you are mine—as I am yours—however either of us tries to writhe away. Because already you are so much a part of me, the cells of my body so saturated with you, every neuron and synapse so magnetized by

you, I couldn't possibly give you up. Nor could you leave
me, I very well know, even if you wished to, even if your
most fervent hope is to obliterate all knowledge of me, all
thought of me, in those moments when I touch you so
completely with my hands and my mouth. I understand
why I must stand naked while you watch me, and why,
when I am facing the white wall and afraid, apprehensive,
shaken, you do not so much as let your body move against
mine. Because if you pressed your body to mine, at that
moment, then I would know that you are helpless, that
your God who is all merciful has once again shown you no
mercy.

But, yes, you *will* make love to me. And I will make
love to you. Over and over. Here, in this miraculously de-
serted apartment, filled only with our wine and our talk
and our endless desire to explore everything about each
other, no matter how hidden or how intimate, our two
bodies flung into the emptiness.

In fact, you have been making love to me for days and
weeks, from the moment we met, often just by looking at
me or talking to me, sometimes touching me, sometimes
hesitating, sometimes devouring me. Easily, too, just going where the spirit leads you, without forethought, because you discovered early on something fundamental
about me, just as I discovered the same about you—no
matter what you say, no matter how much you choose to
hesitate and cover up and lie, to insist that you are des-
tined for sainthood, no matter how, at some final moment,
your body will betray you—you are an easy lay. As I am.
I, at least, admit it. Did you ever think it might be only the
saint, the ascetic, who can be so overcome with desire,

who knows so deeply the power of the voice, the tongue, who knows that someone can be obliterated with a glance?

Because you cannot make love to me in the most ordinary of ways, you are both more docile and more dangerous.

Sometimes when we make love, you have that wild, dark look on your face that is part confusion and part murderous rage, the look that I involuntarily say "No" to, "No, never," thinking that you are going to take me up on my idiot, taunting invitation, that you might back me up against the wall this time, flatten me against it, and calmly and methodically smack me across the face, smartly enough to make me stagger. When you are so dangerous I want to caress you and run from you at the same time.

I will tell you something I've never told anyone before: It takes nerve to go on.

Something else: Every time I step into the street, I expect to get hit by a car, broadsided, flattened into the pavement, or maybe lifted up and flung into the air. I can feel the thud against my body. I'm not looking for it, God knows I don't want it, I am careful and always look both ways, but somewhere, sometime, a car is careening around the corner and my body just happens to be in its way. You told me once you would mow me down like a twelve-ton truck, and I believed you, fully and completely, almost beyond metaphor. Let me tell you, it takes nerve.

So even though sometimes you can have me at your whim and pleasure, submissive to your every breath, there will be times when you are no longer in charge. Then not only will you not walk away, you will be like Jacob wrestling with the angel; you will be lucky to walk at all; you will limp out of here, thanking your lucky stars that someone has finally forced you to your knees. Where you want to be. You should know that now, or later, or whenever I choose, I am going to take you by the shoulders and bend you to the floor, and you will lie there, flat out, so that I can gaze on you and see everything. I won't even have to touch you to overcome you that way; I will wrestle you to the floor by sheer willpower. You will be helpless not to do what I say.

You won't move, you will allow me to touch you and take you however I wish, because, as you have told me, your life is over, you have left everything familiar behind you and you have no idea what will become of you. You don't know any longer what your strength is. Your discomfort and fear make you easy to confuse.

You hate it when I touch you like that, to arouse you. But you desire it, too, because you are made quiet and passive, your will and confusion come to rest, until you close your eyes and let your world darken with desire. At the last moment, I will even probe you and enter you, partly or fully, quickly or slowly, as I really don't mind hurting you, just to see if that violation, that pain, that anxiety, if nothing else, will make you hard and restless. Because sometimes my pain and anger at your impotence need to be dealt back to you. I can press you to the floor, open you, and feel within you your deepest pulse.

You will stammer out that you just want a moment to take a deep breath, to clear your head; you will tell me with your last shred of irony that you'd prefer to be back in your office, settling down to do some serious work. You will tell me that what I am doing to you doesn't feel like love. You are lying, of course. It feels exactly like love. I will hear you and will nod my head sympathetically, all the while continuing to touch you until you can't take it any longer, until you pull me down to you.

Then I am all yours—you can touch me and caress me, you can turn me and bend me as you wish, with your hands, your tongue, your eyes, your voice; I will reach out for you and want you, desperately, even though I am careening into my own land, the promised land, the land you promise me every time we meet here in this empty apartment.

I heard a story once, about a man driving in the mountains after a blizzard, in that whitened, snow-piled quiet, his wife next to him on the front seat and his two small children in the back. A boulder loosened from the mountaintop crashed onto the car, killing everyone instantly—everyone, that is, except the man. The boulder drifted, perhaps, or just plunged; the car followed its own trajectory, and an entire family was crushed to death in an instant, with one life miraculously spared. In the story the man walked away "unscathed." Can you imagine—a man in one second loses his entire family, and he unfastens his seat belt and walks away *unscathed?* Could he have said to himself, Well, thank God, at least *I* wasn't hurt, not a scratch on me?

From the moment you and I looked at each other, from the first moment we spoke, we understood that although we might be spared, neither of us would walk away unscathed.

In my tradition, after being spared imminent death or danger, we are required to recite a prayer of gratitude for survival: *"Blessed are you, Lord our God, King of the universe, who bestows good things upon the guilty, who has bestowed every goodness upon me."* This ancient prayer, taken from the Psalms and called *Birkat ha-Gomel*, befits us perfectly: we both know, every moment we sit together at Sebastian's, every moment in this beautifully empty apartment, that even though we are undeserving we are full of joy. God has indeed bestowed every goodness upon us. He has favored us with blessings despite ourselves and has delivered us, for the moment, from all dangers except for the wild, momentary dangers we inflict upon each other. Whatever happens, we are grateful.

Because this dusty, empty, whitened apartment right now is both our desert and our promised land—the place we have been led to, where every shabbat we eat our double portion of manna. It is bestowed upon us, as a gift, and every week we eat our double portion with gratitude. The ancient rabbis taught that manna in the desert tasted like whatever was most desired; it was infallibly delicious and sated every hunger. So too can we taste upon each other every forbidden and dangerous promise given to a man and a woman—it is there for the asking, the taking, and the taking again, the gift and fulfillment of our sabbath. While it is given to us, before it is taken away.

I will recite the *Birkat ha-Gomel* when you and I have closed the door to this apartment one last time, when the boulder has fallen, when the finger of God has shifted by a fraction and is pointing in some other direction than toward us. In your own way, you will say it, too.

In my tradition, we thank God for gifts bestowed by saying the prayer in the midst of a congregation, among *b'nai Israel*, the children of Israel. In return, the *Gomel* always calls forth an answer. So I will teach the answering prayer to you, also: *"May He who bestowed every goodness upon you continue to do so forever."*

(the apartment)

As they sat up, retrieving their shirts from the floor and buttoning them and then taking long, restorative drinks of water or wine, Nicole mentioned a little sleepily that Tom still hadn't told her about the motorcycle. Well, the car—whatever. Every time she had asked, he had dithered on about sainthood, the pleasures of lying, his childhood, whether or not she believed in the regenerative power of love. Anything but the motorcycle, Nicole pointed out, becoming more alert. Obviously there had been a woman involved—his wife? someone else?

Tom made a stab at straightening out the open collar of his shirt. He looked as if he would straighten his tie if he could, but it was still lying on the floor some feet away, along with various other pieces of clothing neither of them had bothered to put back on yet. He leaned back nonchalantly against the wall. "Yes," he owned up, "afraid so." He was driving late at night, it was a country road, the road was dark, and he'd had a little too much to drink. Quite a lot too much, actually.

That reminded him that making love always left him thirsty, so he poured himself more wine and settled back against the wall. Nicole told him to go on; she sat facing him, hugging her knees and listening intently. Anyway, he continued, he'd hit a tree, and the woman in the passenger seat went through the windshield. They had told him that later; he hadn't known at the time, he had been a little dazed, drunk, of course, and had simply opened the front door of the car and gotten out. Unscathed. It wasn't as if he had exactly forgotten about the woman, she had just sort of melted out of his consciousness; as soon as the car hit the tree he really couldn't remember a thing. It was awful, awful, a terrible thing to do. Unforgivable. They picked him up later, wandering down the road, and by that time there was an ambulance, they were putting her into it, and he suddenly remembered it all, but by then it was too late. They loaded him into a cop car, handcuffed, in the back. Tom clasped his hands together, behind his back, and leaned forward to show Nicole what it was like.

He had vomited in the back of the car; no one paid the slightest attention, and he couldn't do a thing about it, because of the handcuffs. In the police station, when they took off the handcuffs, his wrists were bleeding, maybe from the metal, maybe from the accident, who knows. They had put him into a holding pen, where he had spent the night on a cot, shivering. He had a vague memory that they gave him a Breathalyzer test—which he failed, undoubtedly—and a clearer memory that he was in an agony of uncertainty about the woman; but beyond that, he even now couldn't remember very much.

The next morning they brought him in a police van to the main courthouse, but all things considered, the cops were awfully gentle with him, gentler than he deserved, telling him that the woman in question was fine, hardly injured, just a slight concussion. The only thing was, they would have to photograph and fingerprint him; they assumed he would understand. No one had exactly announced to him, "You're under arrest," but at some point—actually it was in the middle of fingerprinting—one of the cops said casually, "Oh, by the way, technically, you know, you've been arrested." They were quite nice about it, despite everything, decent and thoughtful. When they were finished with the fingerprinting and Tom had scrubbed the ink off his hands—almost off, it was hard to remove—the men shook hands all around, no hard feelings. Tom said, "Thank you," and one of the cops said, "Thank *you*," and then everyone sat down at different desks and filled out a lot of forms, including Tom, who had to list every place he had ever lived in and when and for how long. Then his lawyer arrived, and everyone seemed relieved.

Luckily, thank God, the judge was one of those alarmingly cultured lawyers who knew Tom by reputation and had even visited one of Tom's prize-winning buildings— the opera house he'd done in Toronto. He chatted for a few moments about the structure's classical idiom coupled with the indigenous stone and then had the courtesy to reassure Tom again about the woman. Her family was with her, and she would be okay. Just a fractured collarbone and a slight

concussion. Very, very lucky. But she wouldn't see him, un-
derstandably. In fact, the message was clear that he was
supposed to stay out of the picture. No one was pressing
charges, except the town, for driving under the influence.
He was merely put on probation and sentenced to two hundred hours of community service, which he was supposed
to serve by putting together some mixed-income housing
plans for the town. The judge also suggested, since Tom
was clearly under stress, some form of psychotherapy and
perhaps more involvement in the church he belonged to,
since his lawyer had emphasized his dedication to religion
and generally beneficent character. Creative sentencing,
they had called it. Very soon after that, Tom had heard
Jules deliver a public lecture on the Bible and had sought
him out, and . . . well, Nicole knew the rest.

"Who was she?" Nicole demanded.

Tom was silent; Nicole had to ask again. Finally he
shrugged.

Okay, he said, it was his wife, Elena. They'd been at a
party upstate, where they had started to quarrel, under
their breath, you know how it is, so no one else at the party
could hear. And then it had erupted full blast in the car, as
soon as they were alone. She had been accusing him for
months of not really caring about her, of not even noticing
her existence, and she was right, it was true. She had reminded him that years ago she had been on crutches for
three months, and he'd barely even noticed. Probably he
hadn't. He'd been *en charette*, working around the clock
to meet a deadline. It was true, what Elena said, sadly
true—he had been so obsessed with work that he had had
hardly a thought for anything else. Drunk as he was, he

had been taken aback at her bitterness, all of it, with good reason. So he hadn't had much defense but had put up a good fight anyway, just for the hell of it, because they both had years of anger behind them and because he was so drunk and because he just wanted to fight, and in the middle of it she shoved him and he wrapped them both around a tree. Elena was out of the hospital now and perfectly okay, but, well, she was still hardly speaking to him. He deserved it, of course, that and more. But he had discovered such reservoirs of anger in himself that he could hardly speak to her, either. So he didn't know what would happen. How could you go on, after all that?

"So you can see," Tom said wearily, "you were right all along. My project for sainthood is a shade compromised. Worse than your sabbath. I'm not sure I even want it anymore. Now that everything is over."

Nicole was thoughtful, and sorry for Tom. "It doesn't sound like anything is really over," she said. "You think things are over, but then something happens and it turns out they're not over, after all. Marriage especially. It doesn't seem to end, even if you want it to. It seems to go on, no matter what." Suddenly she sounded grim, grim and a little sad.

Tom disagreed. He really had reached a dead end. In every possible way. His marriage. His work. Also, it was important that Nicole know the worst about him. That he was here as a felon, even though in effect he had walked away unpunished, unscathed. His guilt was undeniable.

Nicole pointed out that he wore the most expensive and elegant hair shirt she had ever come across.

Tom looked startled. "Score one for you," he admitted. "Do you think," he continued, "that the saints were actually good people? Probably not. I suspect there's no connection at all—between goodness and sainthood, I mean. I used to think that saints had to be virtuous, but that's probably just another one of those sentimental myths. Like the picture of Jesus with long wavy hair, looking like a flower child—and he hung out with terrorists!"

"You make them sound like gangsters," Nicole said.

Tom thought about it for a moment and nodded. "My hunch is," he continued, "that the saints were a dangerous breed. Armed. Fanatic. Desperate. Sexually screwed up. Just what you said—expensively dressed gangsters."

He laughed in a very unsaintly way. That was one of the nicest things about him, Nicole thought, that he laughed so easily and that he could flip from laughter to tears in an instant.

"In any case," he assured her, "I seem to be letting go of my sainthood. The sanctimonious version, anyway. It wasn't one of my better qualities."

Nicole wasn't sure which better qualities Tom had in mind, but it was clearly dangerous, sainthood. Not only to the saint. Saints were undoubtedly a devastating lot—gangsters, they both agreed, wrecking normal human life for miles around, no matter how benign and well intentioned they appeared. Tom was undoubtedly one: a gangster with an endless line of credit, a good tailor, and the ability to charm a judge who might nail him for attempted murder.

"Now about that ankle bracelet," Tom continued, grinning and reaching for his tie, which he then knotted swiftly. He stood up and helped Nicole to her feet; it was time for them to go. "As one gangster to another, where did you get it? Who gave it to you? Why do you wear it?"

(the bank)

When Nicole had stopped at the bank a week or so before meeting Tom, she had learned that several hundred dollars in the joint household account she shared with David had been withdrawn, almost to the last penny, that very morning. Naturally she had suspected David, who periodically helped himself to "loans" from whatever source was most handy, no matter the inconvenience to, let's say, Nicole, his dear wife, who might be counting on that money for groceries or the cleaning woman or to pay for Caroline's dance classes. The night of her discovery, Nicole had confronted David about wiping out their joint account, but he had denied it, of course, and two days later, when she had checked at the bank, the money had been mysteriously restored. Nicole had decided not to make an issue of the loss and quick recovery; she would never say a word. If David took their money and then surreptitiously returned the same amount—or near to it— soon after, it was as if he and Nicole were carrying on a conversation, except instead of talking face-to-face, like most people, they did it through illicit withdrawals and deposits in their joint bank account.

The very night she had confronted David about the

mysterious withdrawal of funds, they had made love, at bedtime, with the children sound asleep in their bedrooms down the hall. It had been companionable and sweet, and they hadn't even bothered to turn out the night-lights they had been reading by. David had simply put down his book and reached over to touch Nicole's cheek. Nicole had been willing. "Let's have married sex," she had said, so David had climbed on top of her and entered her without the least preliminary. "Now," Nicole had continued, closing her eyes, "you think about someone else and I'll think about someone else." David had laughed and kissed her.

"I can only think about you," he had whispered into her ear.

Her night life with David was a plus, a credit. Nicole was perfectly aware that, away from the cares of the day, David could be relaxed and loving, warmly generous and attentive. But the sweetness of their night life didn't mean that the debits didn't pile up, too.

So when Nicole checked for taxi fare one day as she and Tom were leaving Sebastian's and found her wallet totally empty, except for some loose change, she was not terribly surprised. Tom suggested that perhaps she had been robbed at lunch, but Nicole knew no robbery had taken place. At least, not in the restaurant. With Tom practically forgotten, Nicole charged into the nearest bank and inserted her bank card into the automatic teller. She pushed the button marked "Balance," and sure enough, the checking account she shared with David was empty again. By now she was livid. And despairing.

She wheeled on Tom. "Marriage!" she said harshly.

Tom grimaced.

Nicole started to walk off, but Tom wouldn't let her. So she told him everything. Distraught as she was, it just spilled out. Her money had simply disappeared overnight. She knew it was David, she just knew it; he had access to it, and it was completely in character for him to wipe her out and not even bother to let her know. He had done it before; in fact, he had done it just a few weeks ago. All during the recitation Nicole looked completely frazzled, almost beside herself, and when she finally wound down, she had reached exhaustion. Who had hurt her the most was one thing; not being able to buy groceries was something else altogether.

"Sorry," she mumbled. "That was more than you bargained for."

Tom understood, he assured her. His own financial situation was more than precarious, as she well knew, but luckily, his wife, despite their mutual difficulties, was the executor of a family foundation, and— He reached into his pocket and pulled out his wallet. "Do you need some dough to get by?" he asked. Even though he had mowed her down like a truck, he could still help her out. Besides, he pointed out with a wry smile, she should remember that she was dealing with a saint.

Instead of taking the money, though, Nicole froze. She looked straight ahead, remembering the price of meals at Sebastian's and how breezily Tom wrote them off with his credit card. "You're out of my league," she said, and strode off.

Tom quickly caught up with her, angry that she wouldn't take his money. It was just a loan or a gift—it didn't matter which—she should just take it, instead of stalking away breathing fire.

"That's just it," said Nicole, "it doesn't mean a thing to you. And if money doesn't mean a thing to you—even when you're not earning any—then you and I live on different planets."

Tom reddened and backed off. "But we do," he said finally, "we do live on different planets. What do you think this is all about? Do you think this is just some ecumenical dialogue?" His voice was rising in a way that Nicole hadn't heard before. "There's no common ground," he pressed on. "You're an observant Jew who guards the sabbath and I'm a fucking saint. You won't give an inch and neither will I."

"I thought you weren't supposed to get angry," retorted Nicole.

"And I thought you weren't supposed to take taxis on the sabbath."

"We won't do it again," said Nicole grimly.

"Yes," Tom assured her, "we will."

(the apartment)

Tom was right: there was no common ground, no ecumenicism. Just one version of sainthood rubbing against another. As the finger of God can reach into a telephone booth, so a spiritual battleground can be a table in a restaurant or an empty apartment.

It was raining out, just pouring, when Nicole unlocked

the door to the empty apartment and stepped in, locking the door behind her and leaving a trail of rain as she walked down the long entry hall. Her hair was sopping wet and hanging in limp strands around her face. She turned and saw Tom, just where she expected him to be, sitting on the floor of the empty living room, his back propped against the white wall. He must have been there for a while, for already there was a paper cup of wine beside him and a book in his lap. He smiled at her and then jumped up, noticing how wet she was.

"You are soaked!" he exclaimed, tipping her chin up and kissing her hungrily.

"Well, it *is* raining out," Nicole answered, kissing him back but trying to be careful not to press her wet raincoat against him.

While Tom kissed her, he unbuttoned her coat, then flung it on the floor. But he liked her wet; he could have devoured her, and Nicole was more than wet; she was soaked to the skin. Finally Tom stepped back. "No umbrella?" he asked.

"I don't carry one," Nicole answered. "Not today, anyway. It's shabbat, remember?" And she explained to Tom that on the sabbath, she wouldn't carry an umbrella, no matter the weather, because it would violate the rabbinic rule about erecting a domicile. It is a little loony, she admitted to Tom, but because there is a sabbath prohibition against putting up a tent as an abode, the ancient rabbis extended the meaning to include putting up any sort of edifice—a house, say, and, by extension, also an umbrella, which goes over your head and protects you from the elements. It makes a sort of odd logic, Nicole assured Tom, who looked as if he might burst out laughing at any second, that on the sabbath an observant Jew like Nicole would not work or tamper with the environment.

"Do you want to remind me again," interrupted Tom, "about how you don't use electricity or telephones?"

Nicole ruffled her hair with her fingers to make it dry faster; she would not, of course, have plugged in her hair dryer today, even if she'd had the foresight to keep one in the empty apartment. Had she known it would pour today, she continued, ignoring Tom's sarcasm, she could have erected her tent—that is, opened her umbrella—one handsbreadth on Friday, before the beginning of the sabbath. In that case, she could have opened the umbrella completely on the sabbath, because she would not have been building an edifice but simply continuing an action already begun. Unfortunately she would not have been permitted to *walk* under the umbrella—in fact, she could not have moved with her open umbrella so much as one step—because, according to the ancient rabbis, that would have meant erecting a new abode at each resting place. Like a nomad in the desert, putting up his tent when his camels and wives and children needed a few days' rest. Okay, end of lesson.

"Why one handsbreadth?" asked Tom, taking shots at kissing her throughout her Talmudic discourse. "And what the hell is a handsbreadth, anyway? What does your legalism tell you about that, rabbi?" He began to unbutton her blouse and was kissing the area around her collarbone.

What Nicole didn't tell Tom—and Tom never asked—was how she had managed to evade her family and get to the apartment in the first place. After all, the Wolfes had usually just been to synagogue together, the whole family, and would normally have gone home for a sabbath lunch. But long ago Nicole had tacitly established for herself the notion that some Saturday afternoons were hers alone, to dispose of as she wished, lunching or walking in the park with her own friends; it was her *shabbat oneg*, her pleasure, after a hectic week. David could give the children lunch and take them to the playground, meeting other fathers on the same schedule. And she could be where she most desired to be: in the empty apartment, with Tom, in Tom's arms.

Soon, though, Nicole shook him off. She hadn't eaten yet and was hungry for lunch. Tom put his arm around her waist, under her blouse, and steered her toward the kitchen, where a large paper bag rested on the counter, all the while whispering into her wet hair something about a handsbreadth, and how much was it, and where could he put it, and would it be worth it, would she like it?

Nicole giggled. "A couple of inches, I think," she said, still wrapped up in his arms, "but I really don't have the faintest idea. It's all stuff I picked up from David. It's what happens when you marry a yeshiva boy. It's crazy, I admit, but I've been doing it for so long, it's practically second nature. Leviticus says, Don't eat shrimp, so I don't eat shrimp. Maybe God really wants it that way—who knows? It's no big deal because I don't adore shrimp all that much, but I wouldn't have minded an umbrella. Pour me some wine, could you, please? All I've had was a little Manischewitz at *shul.*"

Tom released her, and while Nicole unpacked the groceries, he opened a new bottle of wine, poured some for each of them into paper cups, and raised his cup to hers. "Cheers," he said ironically, "or do you want to say your special Hebrew prayer for the wine?" If Nicole were such a law-and-order girl, he certainly didn't want to be responsible for her spiritual demise, for leading her down forbidden pathways into sin.

Nicole grinned. *"Baruch ata adonai eloheinu melech ha-olam, borei pri ha-gafen,"* she intoned, her body swaying. For the fruit of the vine, gratitude.

"And may it be a good vintage," Tom added. "Amen." They both drank, and then Tom slid a container and a plastic fork to her across the counter. "Tuna salad? A roll? Kosher, of course."

"Not if you bought them on shabbat. Sorry."

"No? Well, too bad," said Tom. "What can you expect from the goyim?" He downed his glass of wine and poured himself another. "It *is* legalism, though, you know," he persisted, sharing the container of salad with Nicole and munching on a roll. "I used to think the idea of Jewish legalism was just Christian propaganda. But St. Paul was right, after all. You—you're a walking code of laws. You absolutely toe the line, or some of the lines, anyway. Very interesting." He leaned back against the sink in the empty kitchen and studied Nicole. "I know that you walked here, because you won't ride on the sabbath, and I know that you're not carrying any money, but, ah, how did you make that phone call to let me know that you'd be a little late?"

Nicole hesitated.

"Thoughtful of you," continued Tom, "but how did

you slip around the rules *this* time? Your telephone credit card? Credit cards are okay on the sabbath?"

"You know perfectly well," Nicole answered, finally put on the defensive, "that I was carrying a quarter. One quarter, only one, for a phone call."

"A law is a law," Tom said pointedly. "At least for you guys it is. Or so I thought. Doesn't that bother you? With us, you'd be spending quite a bit of time on your knees—"

"You'd like me to stand up in synagogue, wouldn't you," Nicole said hotly, "and announce that, yes, I am carrying money on the sabbath, and that with my one forbidden quarter I will go to the nearest pay phone to arrange for a little sabbath adultery. You'd like that, wouldn't you?" She downed her glass of wine at a gulp and shivered a little.

"What I'd like is for you to take off your clothes," Tom said. "All of them." And then, when Nicole looked upset and discomfited, he added gently, "You're shivering anyway. I forgot all about how wet you are. You'll be much more comfortable without any clothes on." Taking a few steps back from her, he repeated, "Get undressed. Please. Stand right there against the sink and get undressed."

"Oh, Tom," Nicole began quietly, "I'm cold. I'm hungry. Let's not do this."

"I'll wrap you in a towel," Tom answered, "after a while. And who said you had to starve? Now, take off your clothes."

Nicole slowly and deliberately put down her fork, poured herself another cup of wine, and drank it. She looked thoughtful, pained, as if she were considering how to undress, what to take off first. Tom retreated to the doorway and watched her intently as first she unbuttoned the rest of her blouse and slipped out of it. It stuck to her slightly, it was so damp. She shook it out and placed it carefully on the kitchen counter to dry, next to the tuna salad and rolls.

"Tell me more about your legalism," Tom demanded as Nicole unhooked her bra and took it off. "Is there some sort of rule about taking off your clothes on your sabbath? About eating nude?"

Nicole, unbuttoning the waistband of her skirt, gave Tom a withering look. He laughed, delighted, and raised his cup of wine to her. "You're pretty," he said. "Did I ever tell you?"

Nicole let her skirt drop to the floor around her feet and stepped out of it. She kicked it aside, slipped off her shoes, and began to unroll her panty hose. "Okay," she said in resignation and completely nude, "there. Are you satisfied?"

"I don't know," said Tom, watching her intently. "We'll see." He continued to watch her as she shivered a little. If he were going to get her a towel, wrap her up, and keep her warm and dry, it was not going to be yet. Not just now. For right now, for his pleasure, she could stand still, naked, leaning against the sink.

"I'm freezing," she complained, "and also hungry." She picked up the container of tuna salad, took a forkful, and shivered again. "So, now are you satisfied?"

Tom seemed rooted to the doorway; he was silent, brooding on something. "Tell me more about this legalism of yours," he began finally. "Has it always been part

of . . . ah, your tradition? I seem to remember, from the
Gospel According to Mark, that you legalists caused some
controversy in the first century."

"Are you calling me a Pharisee?" Nicole countered,
narrowing her eyes. "Because if you are, that's okay. For
me it's not a dirty word; all modern Jews are Pharisees."
She folded her arms across her bare chest, trying, as
quickly as possible, to regain the offensive.

"But in *my* tradition, Pharisees are not on our *A* list,"
Tom rejoined. "You remember—you Pharisees didn't
get such great press. It was your legalism," he added
judiciously, "as I recall. In fact—you may find this
familiar—weren't you thought to be a shade hypocritical?
'Whitewashed tombs' I believe was the phrase." Tom
grinned; he definitely enjoyed debating Pharisaism with a
naked woman standing her ground in an empty kitchen.

"I'll tell you about legalism," Nicole said after a
moment, "since you're so hot on it. Have you read
Ecclesiastes lately?" She picked up a roll and took a bite.
Her skirt, shoes, bra, and panty hose were in a little pile at
her feet. She nudged them aside with her bare foot.

"Ecclesiastes? What's that got to do with it? You're
not going to tell me that everything has a season, are you,
and that this is your season for standing around without
clothes on, eating lunch? Give me a break!"

"It's your kind of book, you know," Nicole began casually. "It says that everything fails you—wealth, well-
being, power." She leaned back against the sink and
crossed her legs, knowing that Tom had the whip hand
here but determined to carry on nevertheless, as if they
were just two pals enjoying a weekend luncheon together.

She spooned more tuna salad onto her roll and continued her lecture, seeming to ignore the fact that she was totally naked in front of a fully dressed man who was scrutinizing her minutely.

"Ecclesiastes says, in the end, all you can do is fear God and observe the Commandments. You're right, it is legalism. That means the sabbath. And the dietary laws. No umbrellas, no money, no taxis, on the sabbath. No pork, no shrimp, no Chinese egg rolls. Just fear God and observe the *mitzvot*." Nicole sounded very pure, very sure of herself, despite what Tom was doing to her. If he had these odd fancies, these bizarre cravings to make her jump through hoops, fine, so be it.

"What about the Commandment against adultery?" Tom broke in. "Do you observe that, too?"

Nicole put down her sandwich.

"Adultery," urged Tom. "Thou shalt not. The Seventh Commandment. Heard of it?"

"Oh, God," Nicole begged, finally losing her bravado. "How am I supposed to answer that?" She took a deep breath. "Here I am, on the sabbath, standing in an empty apartment, stark naked, sharing a goddamn kosher lunch with you! And you want me to chat it up about adultery? What do *you* think about adultery? How does it fly with you Christians? What do *you* think the answer is? Why are you doing this to me?"

"For the pleasure of listening to your logic," Tom said, grinning at her. "Because I love to see you like this. Completely undressed and expounding Scripture to me." He thought for a moment. "I suspect what we're doing is what those early Christians had in mind, don't you think?

I mean, when they organized themselves into underground cells to evade the Romans. This is our underground cell, this empty apartment. Fear God and observe the Commandments, is that it?"

"I've had it," Nicole said. "Either get me a towel or I'm getting dressed. What are we doing here, anyway? Is this just some seminar on theology, or—or—are we going to. . . ?"

But Tom couldn't stop. "I know you observe the Commandments . . . well, some of them, anyway—but, okay, what about fearing God? Do you fear God? What *do* you believe, anyway?"

"I don't have to believe anything," Nicole said hotly. "Belief is for Christians, types like you. I'm Jewish—remember? I don't have to believe a thing."

(the apartment)

If you don't believe anything," Tom asked reasonably one sabbath afternoon, "why do you go to synagogue?"

"I go for the wine," Nicole retorted. "My weekly shot of Manischewitz. Really. I get this craving every Saturday for a bit of grape syrup, served in a dentist's little paper cup."

"How interesting," Tom observed mildly, and then he got an ironic look on his face that meant he was about to zero in on Nicole. It was one of the ways they made love: Tom would nail her, or try to. He would do it with the best will in the world, seemingly, in utter good cheer and friendliness, but he would pursue her, if he could, into some disastrous admission.

Once, at Sebastian's, Nicole and Tom were having one of their endless lunches, talking over whether or not Miriam in the Book of Numbers deserved the punishment God gave her, of having her body turn leprous. Maybe that was something wonderful, Tom thought, mulling it over, and not really a punishment at all, something miraculous, a sign. Nicole thought Tom's theory sounded altogether too, well, Christian. He pointed out that God had turned Moses into a leper as well—just his hand, though—as a sign that he should prophesy to the Israelites.

Deep in conversation and without missing a beat, Tom took Nicole's hand and brought it under the table, cradling it in his own. It made Nicole happy to have Tom touch her, secretly, hidden by the tablecloth where no one could see, to have him covet her and claim her. To lead a perfectly ordinary public life of perfectly ordinary conversation, when all the while their bodies were speaking to each other differently, privately, hidden from the outward world. Would her hand whiten, she wondered, like Moses' hand, to show that she was the chosen one? Or would her body become like Miriam's, leprous, a sign of her deviance? For a moment she was tempted to withdraw her hand from Tom's, but she did not.

Once Tom held her hand under the table, once he had it captive, he sometimes liked to position it inside his own in such a way that, suddenly, without warning, he could press something sharp and pointed into her soft flesh. When she couldn't endure it any longer, she gasped and tried to jerk her hand away, but Tom held on. When he released her, a moment later, Nicole was pale and dizzy. But Tom hadn't faltered. "Do you think," he was saying, "that prophecy is like leprosy, somehow—that it puts you in some special high-risk category? I mean, when your hair sizzles and flames come out of your mouth. Prophets are type A, don't you think—shouldn't they have to pay higher premiums?"

Tom did it again and again—claimed Nicole's body publicly, but in such a way that no one could see. Then he would slowly drill the soft flesh of her hand until she couldn't bear the pain and would moan quietly, so that only Tom could hear. Anyone would have thought that they were just clandestinely holding hands, the way lovers did, but if you watched Nicole closely, you would see her turn pale, as if she were about to faint. She never stopped him, though. Afterward they were both dizzy, a little sickened.

In the empty apartment, Tom considered Nicole as she denied that religion counted for anything in her life. "I think you're right; it is a craving," he said judiciously. "But not for wine. I think you mainline a little God, don't you, without admitting it."

"The opiate of the people," Nicole agreed cheerfully without committing herself.

"I doubt it," Tom said dryly. "It doesn't seem to slow you down."

Nicole shrugged, conceding that Tom had scored a point. He was right, she had to admit it; religion was hardly an opiate for her—it was abrasive and demanding, as he very well knew.

"And you pray, don't you," persisted Tom. "I know you pray, because you've told me. You pray at bedtime, with your kids—"

"Only Jake," interrupted Nicole, "and that's because of his religion teacher. He has a pious teacher. It's not me."

"Okay, okay, only Jake, but you pray in synagogue— *shul*, pardon me—don't you? What else would you do in synagogue but pray?"

"You think it's like church," Nicole observed, "but it's different." She thought it over. What *did* she do in synagogue, anyway? And if it wasn't prayer, what was it? "No, I don't pray, not in the sense you mean it, to God. Or, if I do, I do it in Hebrew, so I don't have to know what I'm saying." She laughed at how ludicrous she sounded, but she was serious nevertheless. "You're the one who prays, I bet. Our Father who art in heaven, and all that sort of thing. Not me. I just do the liturgy. It's different."

"Yes, I do pray," Tom admitted quietly, "but I think you do, too. I don't mean to be ecumenical about it, but I'll bet that you're a closet believer. Different cults, but I bet you have some belief."

Nicole looked at Tom quizzically. When Tom admitted that he prayed, when he told the truth about it, it made her feel queer. It was like imagining him roped and bound, thinking of him on his knees, praying. She had once gone with Tom to church, to a place called St. Stephen's Episcopal, and although it wasn't a bastion of the low-church fundamentalism that Tom had grown up with, it was a church he had gone to for years, since coming to New York, he had told her. He felt at home there. "Or at least I'm beginning to," he explained as they entered the

church and found an empty pew toward the rear where no
one would pay attention to them. "For a long time I was
just trying to pass." But by now he had mainstreamed
himself into high-church Episcopalianism, Tom went on
wryly, as befitted an architect of his status. After all, he
said, grinning, it was a little hard to network with potential clients while you were rolling on the floor and speaking in tongues. Not to mention that most of those
low-church types back home didn't renovate cottages in
Southampton or need an architect to design a modernist
barn on the dunes. Nicole skimmed the brochure the usher
had handed her at the door when he had welcomed them
with a hearty smile. The brochure was all about soup
kitchens. Bosnia. A film festival for teens. AIDS. And
something about soap that made no sense to Nicole at all;
the shower ministry, it was called. Despite that, she noted,
agreeing with Tom, the clientele at St. Stephen's looked
like the sort who would enjoy chatting with the nearest architect.

Tom, however, by this time had turned pious. He stu-
diously found the opening hymn in the hymnal, marking
the place with his finger, and he and Nicole stood up as the
procession of ministers and choir entered the church and
walked magisterially down the center aisle. Tom, at least,
began to sing.

Nicole was relieved to learn that when she accompa-
nied Tom to St. Stephen's she didn't have to worry that he
would do something embarrassing, something that would
make her uncomfortable. But she hadn't counted, quite,
on communion. The church got hushed and expectant;
there was a kind of tension in the air, as if now, at last,

worshipers were finally getting down to business. Nicole
sat quietly while Tom rose from the pew and left her to go
to the front of the church. When he returned from the
communion rail, he didn't look at Nicole at all but knelt
beside her, almost as if she weren't there, folded his hands
like a child, and bent his head to pray. In *his* tradition, he
had seven minutes of divine grace, and Tom took all seven
for his prayer, gesticulating slightly with his hands as if in
serious conversation with God. He prayed as if he were explaining something and God was listening, asking questions.

Enclosed in his prayer, explaining things to God, Tom
was submissive; he looked as though he were dying a little, given over to his private colloquy with his king and his
redeemer. Nicole stayed stationary in her pew, mesmerized; she felt like a voyeur. Because Tom seemed so vulnerable then, so bruised, it made Nicole want to hurt him
more, to chasten him, secretly, invisibly. The way he hurt
her, invisibly, under the tablecloth in their restaurant—
she wanted to deal it back to him, here in this hushed
church where Tom bent to pray as if his submission were
the most natural thing in the world. When he got up from
his knees and sat again in the pew next to her, he still
looked a little ashen; he was very far away from her, very
close to God and to the body and blood of the Lamb of
God, Jesus Christ, *which taketh away the sins of the
world.*

Nicole knew that Tom was untouchable in those minutes of communion and divine grace, enclosed in his praying, in his belief, as she was herself sometimes, despite her

skepticism. She felt wonder that Tom allowed her to watch something so deeply private, this praying, something unspeakable. They both knew that prayer, whatever it meant, in whatever language, wrenched you apart, left you overcome and open. More open than sex.

(at home)

When Nicole checked her wallet to pay for groceries one day, she noticed that her MasterCard was gone. That's weird, she thought, I haven't used it lately. Even stranger, the American Express card she also carried was still right there in her wallet, intact. Anyone wanting to steal a credit card, or so she thought, would have taken both of them, no? The thief—if there was one—wouldn't have gone through her monthly financial statements to find out on which card she had the most credit or the lowest interest rate and thus choose MasterCard, would he?

Nor did Nicole believe she had misplaced the card; it just wasn't like her. She was meticulous, even rigid, about not losing or rearranging things that should, she thought, be placed in a certain order. She always dropped her keys in an ashtray on a table beside the front door, so they were always right where she wanted them when she went out. Not for her were the frantic last-minute searches for keys or eyeglasses, the yelping, "Has anyone seen my house keys?" that David indulged in while she stood quietly by, saying, "Have you looked in the ashtray where they belong?" Her silverware was arranged in the drawer in the same order as it was placed on the table: salad fork, dinner fork, knife, spoon. The silverware drawers themselves were carefully marked "Meat" and "Dairy" in accordance with the demands of Jewish dietary laws, that there be a separation between them. She even color-coded the dish towels and sponges: the blue-green end of the spectrum for dairy meals and the red-orange-yellow end for meat. There was nothing in rabbinic law, as Nicole knew, that said you had to use a green sponge to wipe up after macaroni and cheese and a pink sponge after hamburgers, but she was, as the ancient rabbis said, building a fence around the Torah. She did more than was necessary so as not to violate the practices she understood as obligatory. Driving her car, she observed the speed limit even when it was fifty-five, and she didn't pass over a solid white line. She walked on the green and waited on the yellow. So it was not like her, it was not in her nature, to lose a credit card.

She could not say the same for David, however. Not only did he constantly misplace keys, eyeglasses, his watch, and laundry tickets, but he violated other rituals of order as well. He carelessly disregarded the laws of *kashrut*, for example, in his haste to accomplish twelve things at once. He would grab a dairy sponge to wipe up spilled gravy or take a knife out of the meat drawer to spread cream cheese on a bagel. The sponge would have to be thrown out and the knife put aside for twenty-four hours and then thrown into a pot of boiling water. If *kashrut* means anything to you, she would shout at him, waving the knife, then think before you grab something! Just think, for God's sake! People have been doing this for five thousand years! When they were in the desert, they didn't use their goat knife to ladle their yogurt, goddamn it! And Nicole would ostentatiously lay the knife on the sink until she got a chance to make it kosher again.

Her husband's violations of *kashrut* were irritating, but when he broke laws outside the house he was downright dangerous. He drove like a fiend, for example, and boasted about once having driven from Washington to New York in only three and a half hours, doing eighty and never getting caught. Yellow lights to David didn't mean slow down; they encouraged him to speed up in hopes of beating the red. When he once drove through two red lights in a row, he was stopped by the police and had his license revoked, but that didn't deter him at all. He simply continued to drive, but without a license, never even bothering to find out how to get his license reinstated. Nicole was frantic about that, but helpless to prevent him. "What if there's, God forbid, an accident?" she would say. "What about the insurance?"

"Fuck off," David would mutter, "it's my decision."

"You can't drive with the children," Nicole would warn, but David drove the kids around anyway. "What am I supposed to do about your driving car pool?" Nicole would demand in a fury. "Call every parent and say, Oh, by the way, David is driving your kid to school without a driver's license, but don't worry, he says it's okay?"

Yet Nicole got in the car with him anyway, while he drove; she just gave up trying to change David's ways, it was too tiring. Once while David was driving without his license and Nicole was sitting in the passenger seat next to him, he made some outrageously illegal maneuver and right away got himself picked up by the traffic cops. Nicole was furious. "Sit tight," David instructed, getting out of the car to meet the police standing up, "do what I tell you." So he explained to the police that yes, he was driving without his license, he had mistakenly left it home, but his wife was pregnant and when he had asked her to take the wheel, she had complained of nausea.

The cop stuck his head through the car window. "Are you all right, ma'am?" he asked.

"Yes," Nicole answered, smiling weakly and trying to look as if she were about to throw up. "I'm okay, thanks, just—a little—kind of—not feeling well."

She staggered delicately out of the car. Leaning against the side as if she might faint at any moment, she said to David, "Please, how much longer, do you think?"

"Just a minute, honey," he said, flashing her an affectionate smile, "we're just finishing." The cops nodded reassuringly.

A few minutes later the police pulled away and David slid back into the driver's seat. He hadn't even gotten a ticket. "You goddamn bastard," Nicole said furiously, "I wish they had thrown you in jail."

So when she noticed her credit card was missing, she was pretty sure David had taken it. As he liked to say about himself, he occasionally borrowed things on a long-term basis. He enjoyed doing that; it was a challenge. He borrowed books that way, from bookstores, and small items like pitchers and spoons from hotels and restaurants. Once he outdid himself and walked out of a restaurant with two cups and saucers, a milk pitcher, and a little tray—practically a whole tea service. A lovely one, too, David pointed out later, Limoges, what more could you ask for? Nicole was appalled. She felt as if she were aiding and abetting a criminal, or at least a petty thief. But what wife would turn in such a husband as David Wolfe, an award-winning film producer, an intellectual beacon in the arid wastelands of television, for stealing a porcelain teacup?

Nevertheless, the theft of her own credit card was a different story. She hoped that if David had in fact "borrowed" her credit card, it would not be on his usual long-term basis but would just be a short-term crime and wouldn't cost her too much money when she had to pay the monthly bill.

First, though, she retraced her steps of the last week, just in case she had used her card and uncharacteristically left it in some shop or restaurant. Really, though, she had made only one purchase that week, from a bookstore, and when she checked on that, the salesperson remembered her perfectly well but didn't know a thing about a lost credit card.

That night Nicole casually mentioned to David that her MasterCard was missing. "Really?" he answered in a tone even more casual and bored than hers. "Did you leave it somewhere?"

"I checked," she said, "and besides, it's not like me

to." David shrugged and picked up a book. "You didn't go through my wallet, by any chance," Nicole finally challenged him, "and just, well, *slide* it out?"

David was deeply insulted. "If you can't keep track of your credit cards," he said, stalking out of the room, "maybe you shouldn't have them."

"You stole it, you goddamn thief," Nicole said, following him. "I know you, you've probably used it and forged my name all over town."

"Sick woman," muttered David.

(the campus, midday)

Walking out of their offices, Jules engaged Nicole in the same conversation they had had once before, at the playground, asking caustically if she and Tom were "still having lunch."

"I guess we do sometimes go somewhere," Nicole answered vaguely. "There's this apartment . . ."

"Do you?" Jules murmured approvingly, not believing a word of it. "An apartment?"

"Just an empty apartment. We sometimes meet there."

"What do you mean, empty?"

"It's really empty," Nicole answered. "Not just unoccupied. Utterly, utterly empty."

Jules was walking beside her as she spoke, and she

could suddenly feel his breathing change, as if something had slightly altered the balance of hydrogen and oxygen he was taking in.

"The two of you go to an apartment that's empty," Jules repeated as if he had learned that fact by rote. "There's nothing in it at all?"

Nicole looked at Jules for a second; she was giving him what he had been waiting for, a payback. "Nothing," she said.

Jules shook his head in disbelief.

"Okay," she said in mock resignation. "There *is* something in this apartment, now that you mention it."

"What?"

"A corkscrew."

Jules pulled his breath in sharply, as if he had been punched.

(the apartment)

Tom brought Nicole's face to his, gently, with both his hands, as if he would kiss her. But instead of reaching for her with his lips or his tongue, he told her to open her mouth and breathe. "I'm breathing," Nicole pointed out, looking pained but reasonable. "Guess what, I do it all the time."

"No, breathe deeply, slowly."

"What is this—doctor?"

Just do it, Tom told her, so Nicole breathed, deeply, slowly, suspiciously, as if someone held a stethoscope to her chest, because of course she was breathing, what else would she be doing? Breathe, breathe, she thought, why? Couldn't they just make love—breathing, panting, moaning, chanting, gasping—without thinking about it? Finally Tom explained. He wanted to inhale her, consume her breath, breathe into himself what she had breathed out, to take inside himself what had been deep inside her, the warm, moist air from inside her lungs. Tom was close to intoxicated, his eyes closing, breathing, out-in, out-in, in syncopation with Nicole.

It was not enough for him that he could gaze on her naked, placed immobile against a blank wall. For all that, it was only Nicole's skin he could see, white against white, and the airwaves of her shimmering and trembling. He wanted to take something beyond looking, something from deep inside her, something as free and easy as air, but private, touched by her lungs, full of the cells of her body, deep and hidden. He wanted her spirit, Nicole thought, her *nishmat hayyim*, her breath of life, the breath God breathed into Adam at the moment of his creation.

So Nicole breathed when Tom asked her to. But she kept a wary eye on him.

One day he suddenly appeared in the bathroom after her, when she, thinking herself entirely alone, was sitting on the toilet, urinating. Without a second's hesitation,

Tom knelt in front of her, pried open her legs, and thrust his hand into the warm stream. It all happened so quickly that Nicole didn't even have a chance to become horrified, to look up and say, Oh no, sorry, not this, not on your life, so without a word she finished up, washed her hands, and left the bathroom to dress, while Tom was still kneeling there on the floor. Afterward, when she thought about it, she was appalled and would close the bathroom door after herself, carefully and deliberately, even noisily. But some point of honor, or absurdity, kept her from actually locking the door against Tom. After all, if you are exchanging carbon dioxide with someone, delicious as it might be, breathing out just so that he can breathe in, why draw the line at the bathroom door? Where *would* she draw the line? Nicole wondered.

Once when Tom was tenderly holding her in his arms, Nicole had a sudden impulse to murder him. Just that— murder him, quickly and savagely, getting it over with. In her mind, she had drawn back her leg and shoved her knee as powerfully as she could into his groin; she had thrown him to the floor and was stamping on him with all her might.

She didn't breathe a word of this to Tom. On the contrary, she made herself even more pliable and loving to him, as if she were content to give herself over to him completely. But in her imagination Tom was on the floor, half conscious, moaning, while Nicole leaned over him, holding him down, banging his head against the wood, again and again.

Where *would* she draw the line?

(a long time ago, at home)

The cleaning woman is here today," Nicole had said, opening the front door to her apartment. "And the super is working in the second bathroom. There's a leak." She hadn't bothered to say hello, nor had she looked through the peephole when the doorbell rang; she had simply opened the door, knowing who it was who would walk in.

Jules strode in, shut the door behind him, and flattened Nicole against the wall of the foyer. For a second he shoved his tongue into her mouth. As he let her go, he brushed the back of his hand across her breasts. Paying no further attention to her, he walked into the apartment, dropped his briefcase, took off his jacket, and finally turned to Nicole, still without saying hello.

"The cleaning woman?" he asked. "*And* the super? A banner day in the Wolfe household, isn't it. Have you got some coffee?"

"On the stove," Nicole answered. "Come into the kitchen. I'll warm it up."

But Jules stopped her for a moment, reaching out for her as she started for the kitchen. He touched her hair gently in belated greeting and then followed her into the kitchen, where he perched at the kitchen table.

"You okay?" Nicole asked him as she poured two cups of coffee and passed him the carton of milk. "You seem a little strung out this morning."

"Exhausted," he said glumly. "Furious. Martha

kicked me out of bed again last night. She barricades the door against me. I think she piles furniture against it. Unbelievable. Of course I can't get back in, but neither can the kids when they wake up in the morning. Both of them were up at six. Sam climbed in bed with me—the couch, that is—and I'll say this for the little guy, he's got strong legs. Kicked the shit out of me. Meanwhile Jesse wanted breakfast. And of course Martha didn't do a fucking thing. She didn't even come out of her bunker until the kids had their backpacks on."

"Do you want something to eat?" asked Nicole, sliding a basket of rolls left over from breakfast toward Jules.

"What's that?" he asked, eyeing the rolls as if they might be grenades about to blow up in his face. "Oh, yeah, sure. Haven't had anything since Frosted Flakes at six-thirty." He polished off a roll and gulped down some coffee, glaring into his cup. "You make good coffee, you know. I don't know which I depend on more, your coffee or your cunt. By the way, what happened to you this morning? The plaster in the bathroom coming down again? Is Carlos in there? You and David have another fight?"

Nicole said something dryly about it not being multiple choice, so yes, all of it was true, and then she rested her head in her hands and rubbed her eyes in fatigue. Sometimes your house of cards collapses first thing in the morning, she thought, sometimes later in the day, but it always collapses in one fashion or another; that seemed to be the first rule of married life, more graven in stone than the Ten Commandments. The trick to running a household with little money was to stave off the inevitable chaos for as long as possible.

Nicole's one-day-a-week cleaning woman walked in and nodded at Jules.

"Hi, Lusenka," he said grimly.

"Bedrooms first or kitchen?" Lusenka asked Nicole in heavily accented English.

"The kitchen," Nicole answered. "We'll be out of here in a few minutes. I think we'll be using the bedroom to prepare our classes." Then, turning to Jules, she added, "You've brought those commentaries on Job I asked you for, haven't you?"

"Kurwa mac!" exploded Lusenka in Polish, throwing up her hands. *"Kurwa jego mac!"* Good Lord, she was saying, I can't believe this. Again?

"Uwazaj, Lusenka," said Nicole, warning Lusenka to be careful. *"Dobrze?"*

"Dobrze," answered Lusenka. Okay.

"Dziekuje, Lusenka," Nicole said gratefully as Lusenka left the room.

"What did you say to her?" Jules asked suspiciously.

"Oh, nothing," said Nicole. "Actually, I told her that I'm going to fuck your brains out in the bedroom for the next hour, and I don't want her barging in. So she might as well start on the kitchen."

Jules looked glum, as if what he really needed were another cup of coffee.

"Did you tell her you'll fuck my brains out—what's left of them after last night and this morning—before or after we get some work done? And, by the way, just out of curiosity, why do you carry on this way in front of that poor woman?"

"You are a pious lad, aren't you," Nicole answered. "Okay, Job it is. Where would you like to begin—boils, drought—"

"I'm getting the books," interrupted Jules, draining his coffee and standing up. "Did I ever tell you the story about the woman and the six scholars?"

Nicole stopped him by hooking her fingers through his belt. "Listen, Jules," she said, "after the morning you've had, I wouldn't want you to study with me until you have a clear head. I strongly suggest you go into the bedroom and take off all your clothes. All."

Keeping her hand firmly hitched to his pants, Nicole stood up and looked him straight in the eye. One of the things she liked most about Jules was that they were the same height; she could face him squarely, head on. Something else she liked about him was that he had seen the prophet Elijah. On the New Jersey Turnpike. Jules had been driving calmly along—it wasn't even late at night, and he certainly hadn't been drinking—and all of a sudden his car had been sideswiped by a white Cadillac that appeared out of nowhere. Jules had grabbed the wheel with all his might and, *baruch ha-Shem*, just missed being run off the side of the highway at top speed. As he had righted his car, still driving with great caution and pretty shaken up, not to mention angry, furious, he had glanced beside him, and there was the white Cadillac, bright as day, still cruising right alongside him. But this time he got a good look at the driver, and sure enough, it was Elijah himself, the prophet Elijah, bearded, in a blue robe, looking as if he were any second about to ascend into heaven. Then Elijah stepped on the gas and the Cadillac sped out of sight. So Jules knew, as everyone should know by the appearance of Elijah, that the Messianic Age was upon him—indeed, it is upon all of us—and that we should all do good deeds, *tikkun olam*, to repair the world in order to hasten Elijah's reappearance and to hasten the imminent coming of the Messiah.

The best thing about Jules was that he needed her, badly. As much as she needed him. She shook him gently, by his belt. "I want you naked," she added.

"And you?"

"As soon as I clear away here," she answered, releasing her grip on Jules and beginning to put the coffee cups in the sink. "And check on Carlos. Don't worry, he won't come in. Anyway, in the bedroom, my love, or your ass is grass. I promise."

Jules paused for a moment. "You're right," he said slowly. "I *am* strung out this morning. You are, too. Obviously. Just hold me for a minute, could you? You can rough me up all you want in the bedroom. But just hold me right now, okay?"

Nicole stopped what she was doing and took Jules in her arms. It was funny, she thought, current ideology had it exactly backward. She was prey to complex and perverse desires, while what Jules really wanted was to caress and cuddle. He wanted affection, a woman to hold him, to cradle him gently in her arms, a woman to soothe him and pour his coffee. Nicole suspected that he sometimes didn't want sex at all; it was just the price he willingly paid for the coffee and the affection. "You're okay," she murmured to him gently, caressing him and keeping him in her arms. "We're together, that's what's important. We'll look at the stuff on Job later, and if you really didn't sleep last night, you can take a nap while I work." She sighed. "I really do have to prepare that lecture," she added.

"I am so needy for you," Jules said, choking up for a second. "Tell me why you're so tense. You and David really did have another fight?"

"Oh, yes," Nicole answered wearily, letting her body relax into his. "Just a stupid one, as usual. He couldn't find his damn watch, of course, and he accused me of hiding it—it's so stupid. And then, all these people around . . . " She rested against him while he stroked her back. Perhaps, she thought, perhaps she could use a little gentle affection herself.

"Come," Jules said, "head off Carlos so that he doesn't interrupt us, and we'll make love."

A few minutes later, when Nicole opened the door to her bedroom, Jules was lying flat on his back on the floor, his arms crossed behind his head, stark naked. "Good for you," breathed Nicole, closing the door and locking it against the maid and the super and then lying down beside him. She touched his chest lightly and began to run her fingers up and down the side of his body.

"Get undressed," said Jules, his eyes closed.

"In a minute," she said, "just this for a while." She continued stroking him with her fingers, lightly, over his chest and ribs and down his body as far as she could reach while Jules lay motionless, his eyes closed as if he were asleep. Suddenly he trembled violently, but Nicole paid no attention and continued to stroke him.

"Oh, God," he groaned, "quick, I need you so badly." Nicole leaned over and kissed him lightly on the mouth, then sat up and began taking off her clothes.

A moment later she was naked beside him, kissing him, his chest and stomach, the inside of his thighs. He trembled again, violently, as if he were having a convulsion.

Suddenly he bolted upright and, before she could protest, propelled her onto her back. "I am going to drill you to the floor," he said. "Don't make a sound. I am going to pound the daylights out of you. I've been thinking about nothing else for hours." Nicole made an almost inaudible noise. "Quiet!" Jules ordered.

There was a knock at the door.

"Yes?" Nicole answered weakly. From on top of her, Jules pinned her elbows to the floor to prevent her from sitting up.

"I'm going out, Mrs. Wolfe," said a man's voice with a Spanish accent. "Some special screws. I have to get them at the hardware store. I'll be back."

"That's fine, Carlos," Nicole replied in a louder voice. "See you later. Thank you so much."

"Did you want to come take a look, Mrs. Wolfe?" continued Carlos. "See what I've done to the pipes?"

"No, that's okay, Carlos. Thanks. See you later."

"When you look, don't worry about the hole—I fix it later."

"That's fine, Carlos, thanks a lot. Good-bye."

"Will you be here when I get back, Mrs. Wolfe? Fifteen minutes?"

"Yes. But I'm working now, Carlos. I won't be finished for a while. Just let yourself back in. Thank you. See you later."

"Don't worry, Mrs. Wolfe. The girl will let me in."

"Yes, fine, Carlos. Thanks so much. Good-bye now."

Nicole and Jules waited for a minute or two, listening for the sounds of the super walking away, opening and closing the front door.

"Great!" said Jules. "I'm proud of you, you did that very well. Now, flip over."

"Oh, stop," said Nicole. "Not now, good Lord, not now."

"Over," ordered Jules.

"He's not even out of the building yet," Nicole reminded him, playing for time. "What if he changes his mind and comes back?"

"If he comes back, he'll find you snaked out on your stomach, my penis in your rectum. Pretend like you're having your temperature taken. Now, turn over—"

"Come on, Jules," Nicole pleaded, half turning onto her stomach but keeping herself propped up on her elbows, in case she needed to move quickly, defend herself, "get some sense—not now—"

Jules reached for the jar of L'Oréal Night Replenisher on Nicole's bedside table, and Nicole began to plead in earnest. "Look, Jules, that cream's too expensive—not now—I can't—"

"Would you rather stroll into the kitchen for some

olive oil?" asked Jules, flattening her with one hand and applying the cream with the other.

"Good Lord," Nicole said, and then just shuddered while Jules positioned himself on top of her. Suddenly she gasped. "Oh, no," she moaned, "it hurts—it's too much—stop—"

Just then they both heard footsteps moving toward the bedroom door. There was a loud knock, and Carlos called out, "Mrs. Wolfe, Mrs. Wolfe, could I see you for a minute?"

"A hundred and two," Jules said very quietly. "Take an aspirin and call me in the morning."

Nicole made a noise somewhere between choking and giggling.

"Mrs. Wolfe. . . ?"

"Answer him," ordered Jules, whispering into her ear.

Nicole gagged again and tried to move, but she couldn't; she was pinned and knew it. "Answer," ordered Jules again.

"What?" Nicole replied finally.

"There's another leak, I think, Mrs. Wolfe," called in the super. "Could you come take a look? I might have to make a new hole."

"Whatever," said Nicole, again after a long pause. "Later. I'll come later—"

"Good idea," whispered Jules into Nicole's hair. "I will, too."

"Just—whatever—just do it. It's okay, thank you."

"Good going, Nicole," added Jules encouragingly, "keep it up." Nicole shuddered. Her whole body began to

flutter and tremble, as if it were being combed with electricity.

"I'll show you later, Mrs. Wolfe," the super continued.
"When you get out."

"When *I* get out," said Jules.

The super walked away. They could hear his footsteps
and then the front door opening and slamming shut.

Jules moved his body slightly, on top of Nicole, and
she gagged again. "I'm going to throw up," she choked
out.

"That's what you always say when we do this," whispered Jules, kissing the back of her neck and hair. "Go
ahead, throw up. I don't mind."

Nicole moaned and gasped at his slightest movement.
And Jules, as he moved on top of her, continued his litany
of whispers in a private voice so low that it sounded to her
as if it were coming from under the seas or beyond the
heavens. "I think you're seeing stars," he whispered into
her ear as she writhed on the floor. "What is your name?
Who are you?"

Nicole suddenly clawed and heaved herself free from
underneath Jules. She couldn't do it, she just couldn't, not
this way. The two of them rolled over and over, their arms
locked around each other, struggling. But nothing could
deter Jules now.

"What is your telephone number? Where do you live?
What's your address? What's your Social Security number?" whispered Jules, unable to stop, rocking back and
forth on Nicole's body, wherever he found himself. Finally
he pulled himself away from her, lying next to Nicole on

the floor, while she lay beside him, exhausted, hiding her face in the crook of her elbow. He threw his arm over her body and then leaned over her. "What is your name?" he asked again, gently. "Where do you live? Are you mine? Will you love me forever?"

(the apartment)

When you pray," Nicole asked one day, taking a bite of the tuna salad sandwich Tom had brought, as usual, to the apartment, "do you think 'God'; do you think the word *God* and then pray to it?" She had been reading, she said, about different ways to imagine God and to name him— his feminist name, his gender-neutral name, his kabbalistic name. Since she could barely bring herself to believe in God at all, Nicole was perfectly satisfied with the way her liturgy described him in the *Alenu* prayer—*hu eloheinu, eyn od.* "He is our God, there is none other." Not for her the *Eyn Sof,* the Boundless One, or the feminist *Shekhinah* of divine radiance, and certainly not the God in near proximity just yearning to hear from us. If it was difficult for her to believe in the traditional Jewish God, the normative God, how much more so would it be to pray to a God responding to a specialized clientele? Even if she hardly believed in Him, or believed only with great difficulty, *hu eloheinu, eyn od.*

But Tom, a believing Christian? What did he pray to,

or whom? Did he think *God* when he prayed? Which God?

"Yes, I speak to God," Tom said hesitantly, but with some conviction, as if he'd been meaning for a long time to tell this to Nicole. "I do actually *believe* in God," he said, eyeing her apprehensively. "You know I do. I at least admit it. Sometimes it's a struggle to believe. But I do." He smiled at her. "Want to admit it yourself?"

"But when you pray, is it God?" asked Nicole quietly, remembering Tom on his knees, gesticulating. "And who is God, anyway? For you, I mean."

"When I pray, I talk to God and explain things. I say, 'You see how it is, God, that's the problem.' I assume that God accepts and understands, the way a loving parent does, and that he forgives. Or she, if you like. Or, better yet, they—my God is triune, don't forget."

"Don't you think that's childish?" asked Nicole, not with hostility but because she really wanted to find out what in the world Tom meant, what he said when he was beyond her, unreachable, talking to God. "I mean, a bit too anthropomorphic? Too . . . I don't know . . . understanding?"

"Well, yes," admitted Tom, "but partly that's what I was taught to do. That's the model I grew up with, the parent-child model, and I've never seen any real reason to give it up. I know it's sentimental and Victorian, I know it sounds fraudulent to you . . ."

Tom looked intently at Nicole, trying to make her understand. God as a parent was someone he could talk to, someone who comprehended beyond man's own limitations, someone who loved, always, and would not abandon him. God was always there for him, even if no one else was. God the Father. Our Father who art in heaven, hallowed be His name. Yes, it was anthropomorphic, but that didn't make it wrong, nor did the awkwardness of it diminish his faith. On the contrary, actually. He felt it deeply, that God knew him, even that part of him of which he was most ashamed, and God would forgive. "It's in my hymns," Tom added, "in my liturgy. The parent who unconditionally loves. Who unconditionally forgives."

"Only a parent unconditionally loves. A *real* parent."

"That's what you think."

"I can't believe in unconditional anything—faith, love, forgiveness," Nicole went on, troubled, less sure of herself than she sounded. "For me, it's just not possible."

"But for me, it is," Tom said softly. "That's one of the differences between us. I believe unconditional love does exist, not only from God, but sometimes . . . well, never mind. It just does, that's all."

Nicole was suddenly jealous. Tom's faith seemed so effortless, so sweet and deep, while hers—what there was of it—often left her in shreds. The closer she came to something that might be called faith, the more uneasy and vulnerable she felt. In her tradition, if you approached too close to God, fire would "come out from before the Lord" and destroy you, as it devoured Nadav and Avihu, the sons of the high priest Aaron, when they brought God "illicit fire" with their incense. It seemed to Nicole that whenever she prayed, her offering felt dangerously close to "illicit fire"; God might well and deservedly incinerate her. She would rather take off her clothes; she would rather perform the most perverse and annihilating sexual act than engage in a true offering, a true act of prayer. Sex was easy. It was belief that was hard.

(the apartment)

Many years ago, when she was a teenager, Nicole told Tom when they were both lying about in their empty apartment, she had let a man pick her up on Fifth Avenue. Just like that. He picked her up, she said, by passing by and calling out her name. *Catherine*, he had called out to her. *Yes*, Nicole had said. She became Catherine, and she went with him, strolling along at his side, this total stranger, down Fifth Avenue.

Are you appalled? she asked.

Shocked and appalled, Tom answered. As usual. Then he added, That's about the tenth time this week you've asked me that question. How were you Catherine?

She was sixteen, and it all had to do with towels.

You know those tacky specialty shops on Fifth Avenue? Nicole asked, propping herself up on one elbow. For tourists? Those narrow little stores with windows full of junk—cameras, opera glasses, tea sets, and stacks and stacks of towels? Well, I was just loitering about, looking at the towels.

Tom nodded. For someone who was a bit of an outlaw, he pointed out, loitering about and planning her trousseau must have been particularly dangerous.

They were black, she said, you don't understand. She had never seen black towels before. In her family, when she was growing up, all the towels were either beige or powder blue and matched the tiles in the bathroom. It was the black towels that did it. When the man came by, looking at nothing in particular, he just sort of slowed down near her. Then he really slowed down, and they both stared intently at the black towels. Catherine? he had asked. Nicole had said, Oh, *hi*, and joined him. That's all it took.

And now someone is going to get hurt, Tom said.

Well, yes, maybe.

I became the girl he wanted me to be, Nicole said. I knew perfectly well that he didn't really think I was someone named Catherine, but I became her anyway. Whoever she was. And then I went off with him.

Where did you go? asked Tom. The tea room at Lord & Taylor?

Well, first we walked for a while, down Fifth Avenue. Just talking—do you want me to go on?—while he claimed he remembered meeting me somewhere, and I just more or less agreed to whatever he said. Can you imagine how dumbfounded that poor guy must have been? Picking up some teenager who played along with his whole pathetic story? I told him everything he wanted to know, where I went to school, what my parents did, how I had always wanted to be a racing-car driver. Absolutely everything. It got easier and easier. Catherine kind of took over.

So you just walked around and talked? Like chums?

Not exactly. . . .

Gangsters

So?

When we got to Forty-second Street, he asked me if I would like to go to the movies with him. I figured Catherine would do something like that, so I said yes. Of course, by this time, we were old friends. . . .

Of course.

I remembered piles of things we used to do together, how we used to go to the movies, take long walks, tell bad jokes, drink chocolate milkshakes. He asked me if I still adored French fries, so I really thought it over and said, Well, yes, but probably not as much. I think I must really have missed him when I didn't see him all those years.

We found a movie theater, and we went in, Nicole continued. It was almost completely empty; it was as if we had the whole theater to ourselves. So he found seats for us in the exact middle of the theater; we weren't hiding in corners or anything. I thought it was wonderful, a whole movie house, all for us. I can't remember what the movie was. All I saw was a man leaning over a pool table, with a long stick in his hands. You could see his craziness, how crazy he was to play pool.

Nicole stopped. Then it got really awful, she said.

No kidding.

He took my hand. At first I thought he just wanted to hold it. I didn't much want him to—actually, by this time he kind of repelled me, and I was sorry I had come. But he held on to my hand, tightly, much too tightly. Put it across him. I had never felt a man before, he was stiff and hard. He seemed enormous. Hot, too. He was burning. My hand was burning. When I tried to jerk my hand away, he just held on to it harder and pressed it against him. I thought,

Here I am in this enormous theater, and there's no one around. This man is an utter stranger. He could do anything he wants to me, and no one would save me. I panicked, but for some reason I didn't say a word. I didn't tell him to let go, I didn't scream. In fact, I kept watching the movie. And it was always Paul Newman leaning across a pool table, looking crazed. And the man next to me obviously crazy, too.

And then he leaned over. Started whispering things to me, like *Could I feel him?* and *Did I want to go down on him?* I said things like *No, thank you* and *Please, can't we just watch the movie?* I was just frozen to my seat, I didn't take my eyes off the screen. Finally he let me go. For no reason. He let go of my hand, and I leapt up and raced out of the movie theater. I remember running and running. Back up Fifth Avenue, past all the stores I had looked into. Just running. At full speed.

Tom watched her, as if he could see her running.

The next thing I remember is washing my hands. Washing and washing and washing. When I was finished washing my hands, I took a shower and shampooed my hair. And then I washed everything all over again.

Nicole suddenly looked very prim, like a well-brought-up sixteen-year-old from a home of powder blue towels. She sat up very straight, with excellent posture.

Give me your hand, Tom said.

I don't think I want to, Nicole said uneasily. If you don't mind. It occurred to her that here she was, in an empty apartment, with a man she hardly knew, who could do anything to her.

No, she insisted again, while Tom waited. He was

silent, and so was Nicole. Nicole tentatively held out her hand.

One of the dangerous things about you, said Tom, holding her hand, is that you tell the truth. Even when you're lying.

I always tell the truth, Nicole said primly. I never lie. But you—you lie all the time.

Benign lies, said Tom. Only benign lies. Small potatoes.

That's much more dangerous, Nicole continued uneasily.

No, Tom disagreed, your truth telling is much more dangerous than my lies. No contest.

Make love to me, Nicole begged. Or—I'll make love to you, like the stranger. Whatever you want.

Tom paused, ominously, still holding Nicole by the hand. She was very still, waiting. He certainly would not place her hand over him, like the man in her story; it would be entirely unlike him. Perhaps he would simply take her hand and kiss it. More likely he would burn her somehow, not the way the stranger did, but with some flame of his own on her flesh, some scarring, until she was sick with the pain of it. For telling the truth, Tom would say. For not admitting how dangerous that is. I like stigmata, Tom would say. On you, that is.

Then he would take her with his tongue, teasing her with it, pressing it into her while he held her naked body to the floor with his hands, his weight, so that she arched under him, struggled and fought and came, again and again, until she was exhausted, almost weeping. When finally he let her go, she would curl up like a child, still breathless, vacant, as if he had taken some deep part of her, like a lozenge on his tongue, and swallowed it.

(the apartment)

You asked me what it is like for a woman to have an orgasm. I don't know, I wish I knew. I have never made love to a woman. I've never watched women making love, even. I wish I had. So I am as curious as you are, about women. All I know is what it is like for me to come, and all I can tell you is that it's awful, that each time it happens I hope it never happens again. I am completely obliterated by it. I have no self, no integrity; it simply sweeps me away into a kind of nothingness of self that is horrible. I am terrified of orgasm, and I will delay it as much as possible, sidestep it, pretend it is not there and cannot possibly happen, until I am swept off by it, until it overtakes me, and then it is just horrible. Then I am lost, elsewhere, some place where there is no *me* and no *you*, where neither of us has any existence, where certainly there is no love, not that love makes any difference. It is just a place to be lost in, until gradually, very gradually, I can begin to be myself again.

When it begins, it is not so much terrible as humiliating. Humiliating because I know what's coming, and I can't control it or stop it. My body has just taken over, it moves in a way that's asking for something, but what it's asking for is anguish. Nevertheless, it keeps asking. In fact, it keeps begging for it and won't give up. So, for a while I'm just outside my body, looking on, watching it go through that swaying and rippling, watching it beg for more, and I begin to be horrified. Because the body that I'm watching, and that I'm feeling, just won't stop. It can't; that's the nature of sex. That after a while you don't even want it to stop, no matter how awful it is. You don't even care anymore. You are transfixed by a power that you can't see or name, but a power that simply picks you up and dangles you by a thread in the darkest reaches of the universe.

So by the time I begin to come, I am already lost. So I come, and come, and each time it's worse than the last, and I think I simply can't bear it anymore. It's not that I'm thinking these thoughts in words; in fact, I have no words any longer. If you were to ask me my name, even, I wouldn't be able to tell you. Not only because I don't have the word for my name, but because I don't any more have a name. It's gone, along with everything else about myself that I ever knew. But I couldn't possibly in the middle of sex explain this to anyone, because talking is impossible, and anything I might try to say would be like sound particles having no speed or direction. All I can do is gag and think I am going to throw up. Really. I'm sorry, but I'm afraid I might throw up.

But you cry. You don't throw up. Sometimes you cry.

Yes, sometimes, but even crying I can't do for a while. Until the climax is mostly over, and I am just faced with the memory of how far beyond myself I am. Then I can cry.

What are you crying for, do you think?

I cry for myself and how utterly lost I am. What I most want, then, is to cry and perhaps to be held. But what I really long for, lost as I am, is my mother.

After I've come, the person I most want is my mother.

(the rapids)

Nicole thought there was no such thing as a benign lie; it was an oxymoron, a contradiction in terms. Only someone like Tom, someone who could hurl his wife through a windshield and then saunter off down the road, drunk or not, still believing he had aspirations toward sainthood, only someone like that could believe in the benign lie. A lie is a lie, thought Nicole, legalistic to the core, just as Tom had said. *She* wouldn't lie. Well, lie outright. Not often, anyway. Certainly no benign lies. And if you won't lie, there's bound to be the occasional upheaval in your life; that's the price of honesty. So sometimes Nicole found herself at the center of a melodrama, because if you won't lie, you give up the option of opportunely sliding away.

But Tom! He lied all the time, didn't he, and probably couldn't tell the difference anymore between lying and telling the truth. At least if she lied, which she would do only rarely and under great duress, Nicole knew she was lying. Tom, however, seemed to think that lies were just another way of hedging your bets, of having it both ways so that you wouldn't have to be *too* hard on yourself. Tom was good at plumbing the depths of his soul, as long as the depths were not too deep and depressing, the scenery was good, and he got some good conversation out of it. Having a perfectly awful time, Tom would call out cheerily from his depths. Wish you were here.

Thinking about Tom's so-called benign lies reminded Nicole of an encounter she had once had with Jules. Jules wouldn't lie, either; he would bruise or get bruised, but, unlike Tom, he was uncomfortable with evasions and deceptions. It had been a sunny Saturday afternoon, a perfect day, really, to enjoy the holiness and leisure of the sabbath by taking the children to the playground for the afternoon. David was away for a few days, in Washington, talking to some legislators about plans for welfare reform and its effect on poverty-level teen mothers for his new documentary, so Nicole's plan was to corral the children, get them to the playground, where they would let off steam outdoors in the sunshine. She would be sure to find some of her own friends there as well. It was a good thing it wasn't raining.

Nicole knew that she would need a cup of coffee at the playground but knew also that she would have to be resourceful about getting one, since it was the sabbath and she wouldn't be handling money. She would have to make the coffee herself but could not actually brew it because that would be a violation of the sabbath prohibition against cooking. No percolators or espresso machines on shabbat. Instead Nicole took a thermos out of her cupboard, rinsed it out with simmering water from the coffee urn she kept plugged in for the twenty-five hours of shab-

bat, and then took from her shelf two coffee bags, like
teabags, that she could use on the sabbath, since steeping
them in hot water would not actually be an act of "cooking." Following the laws of sabbath observance that she
had learned from David, Nicole filled a pitcher first, then
transferred the heated water to a second vessel—the thermos—letting the water cool somewhat and therefore not
"cook," and then she added her coffee bags and a generous splash of milk. This ritual, complicated as it was, gave
Nicole a great deal of pleasure. Like Tom's communion, it
afforded her a few moments of, if not divine grace itself, at
least the satisfaction that came from being law-abiding,
plus of course a thermos full of hot coffee. It wouldn't be
as hot as she ordinarily liked her coffee, but, still, caffeine
was caffeine. Despite all its prohibitions, the sabbath was
not supposed to be about deprivation, Nicole would remind herself, and certainly there was nothing in the Torah
requiring caffeine withdrawal.

Jake, meanwhile, strapped himself into his new
Rollerblades, Caroline stuck her Chinese jump rope into
her latest copy of *Teen Beat*, and the three of them headed
down the street, Nicole with her thermos slung on a strap
over her shoulder.

When she entered the playground, her two children in
tow, she immediately spotted Jules, who waved her over to
a spot next to him on the park bench.

"I had a hunch you'd be here," Nicole said warmly,
enjoying the sunshine, the breeze, the chance to relax with
friends for a bit while her children raced around. Jake had
already attached himself to Sam, quite literally, by bor-
rowing Caroline's Chinese jump rope and tying one end of

it around Sam's waist, then holding on to the other end so that Sam could pull him at breakneck speed. Caroline shouted five minutes, five minutes was it, then she wanted her jump rope back. Meanwhile she would sit apart from her mother and the younger children to check what *Teen Beat* had to say about tweezing your eyebrows. Nicole sat down next to Jules.

"In fact," Nicole continued, "I was so sure I'd run into you, I brought you some coffee."

Jules looked interested.

"The way you like it," Nicole said sweetly. "Light, very light."

"Sorry," said Jules, disappointed. "No can do. I had a roast beef sandwich for lunch."

Jules pointed out the obvious: he would love to have the coffee, but he could not, thank you very much, because he had eaten meat for lunch and therefore was obligated to wait six hours before having a dairy product. Dutch Jews waited only an hour—or was it twenty-two minutes?—and some European Jews let three hours lapse between eating meat and eating dairy, but Jules had the misfortune of having ancestors who had been Russian or Lithuanian or had come from some remote pale or other, where it was the custom to wait six hours. Moreover, for Jules, there was the issue of "carrying." An observant Jew was not supposed to carry anything on the sabbath, although, Jules conceded, that prohibition was interpreted differently under different circumstances. Jules didn't wish to be more legalistic than thou; still, he didn't feel comfortable benefiting from someone else's carrying a thermos when he himself wouldn't have done so. It was Nicole's prerogative, of course; she could do as she wished, and far be it from Jules to gainsay her. Yet he didn't feel right about joining in. Much as he would have liked to. So he was turning down the coffee, and while he was at it, he had to point out that it wasn't exactly in the spirit of the sabbath for Nicole to allow her son to tear around the playground on Rollerblades.

Nicole nodded, sat back, removed the lid of her thermos, poured herself a cup of coffee, and inhaled deeply. She took a sip, then another, breathing in the warm, comforting steam. If she were going to be a single parent for the weekend, rich and absorbing as it would be to spend all that time with her children, she still needed some survival mechanisms, sabbath or no sabbath. Coffee was certainly one of them, enjoyed on a park bench in balmy sunshine, no matter how she managed to get it to the playground or what she had had for lunch.

Jules stared intently at his watch as if he were making some calculations.

"Checking the angle of the sun?" asked Nicole.

"No," he said sourly. He was just calculating something. Let's see, he had eaten that roast beef sandwich at lunch, which he had finished about 1:49 or so; it was now 3:12. So while it was obviously true that the requisite six hours had barely begun to pass, nevertheless twenty-two minutes certainly had gone by after that sandwich, and even some moments more than an hour— Jules took the plastic cup of coffee from Nicole's hand and gulped it down. Then he poured himself another cup.

He leaned back against the park bench, coffee steaming in his hand and a big smile on his face. "I hate myself," he said cheerfully. "I'm such a fraud."

Jules's admission, friendly as it was, made Nicole smile, but it also reminded her of Tom, whom she would not be able to see this weekend while David was away. It was Tom who was truly fraudulent, and in matters much larger than whether or not you took your coffee with a splash of milk. But even though Tom confessed to his own hypocrisy all the time, he was always so charming, so winning, in the sincerity of his self-deprecation, he was hard to reproach. Because he confessed so readily, he made his weaknesses lovable and touching, his benign lying a measure of his honesty, his fraudulence an indicator only of his intense desire to please and be loved.

Thinking about Tom made Nicole want to talk about him, of course, even though Jules was not the safest choice around for casual conversation. Nevertheless she couldn't help it. So Nicole, as if she weren't thinking about Tom at all but rather had the interests of the university, her employer, deeply at heart, asked Jules—casually—about how the plans were going for that addition to the university archives, and wasn't he recommending Tom for the job?

Jules looked surprised. He had nothing to do with it, he said, and besides, why would anyone take his recommendation for an architect, of all things? What did *he* know about architecture? Tom was an interesting guy, but . . . And even if Jules were in a position to recommend architects, ludicrous as that might be, why would he go out on a limb for Tom, who was up to his neck in lawsuits for buildings that were either outrageously ugly or had fallen down? Get real, lady.

Nicole was so taken aback that she stopped enjoying her coffee, put the lid back on the thermos, and sat up sharply to face Jules. Hadn't Tom told her. . . ? But of course Jules was right; it was obvious. Everything he said made perfect sense.

Patiently, as if pointing out something to a dim-witted creature, Jules instructed Nicole not to believe everything she heard. Especially from Tom.

"But he's so sincere," Nicole protested weakly.

"Sincerity is not authenticity," Jules said pedantically, with perfect justice.

One of Tom's benign lies, Nicole realized later. And it didn't even profit him: it was told for the pure pleasure of lying and told probably to make Tom seem more damaged and distraught than apparently he was. Perhaps he *did* need to revive his career as an architect, but certainly not through Jules; Tom's wife, with her private foundation and her family philanthropy, was obviously a much better source of prestigious commissions than anyone in Nicole's circle of friends could ever be and a source that Tom had used in the past. He didn't exactly hide his light under a bushel, his current distress notwithstanding. He just enjoyed his benign lie; he enjoyed parading his distress for Nicole so that she could feel sorry for him, concerned, engaged by this charming and brilliant man skidding helplessly toward receivership. Even more, he enjoyed owning up to it afterward when Nicole confronted him. He had lied, he said, because of course he *wished* he had that job;

it had sounded so appealing to work for a university rather than for someone who had made a killing in junk bonds. But more than that, he had imagined himself as part of Nicole's world; his lie, misguided as it was, was designed to bring him even closer to her and to impress her with the diversity of his talent. He was hardly even abashed. And of course he wouldn't care if Nicole's children were rollerblading on the sabbath. Fun was fun.

Confession, rather than being good for the soul, was part of Tom's arsenal of seduction. Tom would dither on and on about his bad conscience, as if the admission itself somehow exonerated him. He would make himself out to be even blacker than he was, for the delicious effect of it, for show. "You think you can charm everyone, even God, with your devout explanations and stories," Nicole would charge. "For you, a little confession goes a long way." It gave him a thrill to behave badly, she would go on, so that he could seduce someone—his wife, Nicole herself—with a confession of how terrible, how irreparably sinful, he was. He even tried to seduce God, she would maintain, righteously indignant on God's behalf. Even though she found it so difficult to believe in God, it seemed unfair to try to seduce him with overheated confessions.

Yes, it was true; Tom would admit it immediately. In fact, it was even worse than she had thought: he was always hoping that somehow he would get away scot-free, more or less as he had walked away from the car crash when he'd heaved his wife through the windshield. To put the best possible light on it, he was drunk; to delve a shade more deeply into it, he wished his wife dead, even if he himself died in the process. In either case he was guilty, no matter how lenient the judge was. *Birkat ha-Gomel*, wasn't it? God bestowing good things upon the guilty and all that sort of thing, in both of their traditions and mercifully for both of them, didn't she think? As for his wife, despite an occasional drink at a restaurant, which always turned out to be a fiasco anyway, she was punishing him by her continued silence, by her refusal to traffic with him at all. Which suited Tom admirably, he had to admit.

"Don't follow my example," he would say darkly when Nicole charged him with less than saintly behavior. "I'm a great sinner." Then he would look quite pleased with himself; he couldn't help it. After all, he believed not only in the benign lie, but also in the remission of sin. Unconditionally.

That was the whole problem, Nicole thought. In Tom's world he could do constant, unremitting damage, wreak havoc all around him, as long as he occasionally owned up to it and was charmingly, winningly sorry. Not so in *her* world, where being sorry was not enough; one had to make amends. Nicole herself didn't care to admit to wrongdoing, but she did try to make amends, in her own way, or at least to balance out the ledger.

No, Tom would say, life doesn't work that way. He would point out that she was not as straightforward as she liked to think, that she was just as devious in her life as he was. Not without apologies, of course, and shivers of remorse, but, Tom asked rhetorically, wasn't it *her* tradition that prized action and behavior over lip service to a creed?

Where it was not enough to want to change—you had to act on it, openly, make good on your promises? Fear God and observe the *mitzvot*, wasn't that it?

Besides, Tom pointed out, Nicole seemed quite comfortable doing absolutely nothing about her marriage, except for occasional bouts of melodrama and sometimes appearing as if she were about to drown. Very appealing, Tom would say, that drowning look, but not substantial.

Look who's talking, Nicole would retort. She and Tom really were at odds. She persisted in thinking that Tom was much more dangerous than she was, living out his lies, damaging people, and calling it benign. If Tom weren't such a benign liar, he would acknowledge that he wanted a divorce so badly he would even kill his wife, murder her, no matter the cost. If he stopped lying— especially to himself—he would actually have to leave his wife, walk away as he had that night in the country, but this time walk away for good, sober and clearheaded, for his own peace of mind and hers.

But he evaded, he pretended, in the same way that he brandished that silly walking stick, to call attention to himself and to seem vulnerable at the same time. He let people think he was one way, saintly, let's say, or winningly sinful—maybe he even *was* saintly, in some inexplicable way—but, really, he was in the business of saintliness in order to make the quick getaway. In his true reality, the Holy Ghost in himself, he was wrapped in a barrel, going over the rapids. He was a Houdini, she thought, not a saint.

(at home, in the kitchen)

It was late at night and the children were in bed and already fast asleep when David and Nicole were just finishing cleaning up the kitchen after dinner. *Long* after dinner: it had been that sort of night, with the children causing a million last-minute problems, each involving unremitting attention from at least one parent. Caroline had had a crying jag because the tights she had wanted to wear the next day were suddenly too small—no other tights exactly matched the turtleneck shirt she was planning to wear with the regulation plaid jumper that was her school uniform; in fact, all of her other tights were not only too small, too short, too ill fitting, but absolutely, *totally* wrong in every possible way, and it was too late to change her plan for that turtleneck because she had already promised her best friend she would wear it. Caroline had raged and cried so miserably and for so long that Nicole almost cried, too, until David put a stop to it by yelling that Jake had broken his thermos and why the hell didn't they have an extra one around? Finally things had quieted down.

David was putting the last dishes in the dishwasher while Nicole ran a sponge over the table and the countertops. "Tea?" David asked, starting the dishwasher and then filling the teakettle and putting it on the stove. Nicole nodded, sat down at the kitchen table, and rubbed her eyes, dead tired.

Without saying anything, she watched David get out the cups and the teabags. He looked exhausted, too. It was the first quiet moment they had had all evening. David poured the tea, measured out a teaspoon of sugar for Nicole and three teaspoons for himself, and handed Nicole her cup. Then he lounged against the counter, stirring his tea, and began what was obviously going to be a long story about the meeting he'd had late that afternoon.

Nicole, idly sipping her tea, interrupted him. "Do you believe in love?" she asked.

David stopped stirring his tea and regarded her gravely. "Love of one's country? Love for your children? Of course I do."

Nicole said she meant love between a man and a woman.

David drank his tea while he considered the question. Romantic love, he thought, could never last very long, but love between a husband and wife—that was a different story. It was hard, he admitted, you had to work at it and sometimes you'd never guess it was love, but— Suddenly he stopped himself. "Are you asking me do I love you?"

Nicole didn't answer but continued to look at him, her chin in her hands. So David put down his teacup and went over to her, helping her out of her chair and then holding her while she rested against him, her back to his front. They leaned against the kitchen counter this way for a long time, David with his arms wrapped around Nicole, relaxed, quiet. "What is it you're worrying about?" he asked finally. "You know I love you. I still do."

Nicole loosened his arms and turned around to face him. She in turn put her arms around his waist, tightly, bringing him close to her, as close as she could. "Me, too," she whispered, resting against his chest.

(in synagogue, on the sabbath)

Nicole, with David and her children around her, stood up with the rest of the congregation while the Torah, the scroll with the text of the Bible handprinted on its parchment leaves, was carried around the synagogue. The heavy scroll, covered with an ornately decorated velvet mantle, was carried in a kind of casual parade, in and out among the rows of people. *Yours, O Lord, is the greatness and the power and the splendor,* everyone sang loudly in Hebrew. As the man carrying the Torah passed by, people would surge forward and reach out to touch the scroll with their prayer books, or men would extend the corner of their *talleisim,* their prayer shawls. Then they would bring whatever touched the Torah to their lips, in a kind of kiss. Nicole's habit was to stand stolidly apart as the scroll was carried by, her arms folded across her chest, a look of uncomfortable forbearance on her face. She would not kiss the Torah, no matter what the custom was. It was a primitive, pagan rite, she thought, this kissing of books; she would not do it. Bibliophilia, idolatry, that's all it was. Jews had supposedly renounced idolatry centuries ago, and there they went, holding out their prayer shawls for contact with a sacred scroll. The man carrying the Torah paused near Nicole, waiting politely for her to reach out and touch it, but Nicole refused to budge. "Torah harassment," she whispered to David.

David shrugged, touched the corner of his embroidered *tallis* to the Torah, and ostentatiously brought it to his lips. Then he marshaled Jake ahead of him and signaled to Caroline so that his children, too, might touch the Torah with their prayer books, while Nicole stood by impassively. At this part of the service she always thought of Stephen Dedalus slipping into a church during mass and saying to himself, *"Non serviam."* Well, she wouldn't serve, either, not if it meant kissing books and scrolls. She would stand back, look on from afar. Let others do all the ritual bowing and scraping.

Another ritual that drew Nicole's discomfort was the one, at the end of the reading of that day's Bible portion, when someone from the congregation—a husky type, usually—would take hold of the Torah's two wooden handles and hoist the heavy scroll into the air, holding it open so that everyone could see the text. "Pumping parchment," Nicole would stage-whisper to David; Caroline would look demurely shocked and then giggle behind her prayer book. Even sillier, Nicole thought, was that some people had the custom of pointing to the Torah, held aloft in the air, with their little fingers. Then everyone would sing together in Hebrew, "This is the Torah that came to the children of Israel from the mouth of God through the hand of Moses." Innocuous enough, Nicole had to admit, although the words sounded more absurd in English than through the scrim of ancient Hebrew. Sometimes Nicole was sorry that she understood any Hebrew. As she had claimed to Tom, she sometimes preferred not to know what it was she was actually saying. Imagine walking into a room, she thought, a religious service no less, where one person is hoisting a heavy scroll in the air and everyone

else is pointing to it with their pinkies. Any God who
would ask for this, Nicole would point out later, describing the scene to Tom, was exactly the sort of God who
would say, Oh, by the way, do me a favor and pass up the
shrimp at the next cocktail party. This God had a peculiar
sense of humor.

But there were moments when she was moved despite
herself. After all of the readings from the Bible, after the
ragtag processional when everyone (except Nicole) kissed
their prayer books and scrolls, the Torah would be returned to its cabinet, the Ark, for another week. Someone
would slide the large, heavy scroll into place, and then
everyone would stand and sing *Etz hayyim hi lama-
chazikim ba*. "The Torah is a tree of life / To those who
revere its teachings." The melody was mournful and sad,
as if everyone were bidding farewell to something very
beautiful. Skeptical as Nicole was about piety, about what
she thought were the inanities of the liturgy, she would be
moved almost to the point of desperation. It seemed so in-
comprehensibly sad, so full of loss, to close the Torah and
shut it up behind the doors of the Ark. If, as the ancient
rabbis taught, the sabbath is a taste of eternity to come, if
heaven is just the sabbath prolonged forever, then that
moment in synagogue seemed to Nicole to signal the end
of the sabbath and thus the end of what she knew of
heaven. It was as if she had been given a sliver of heaven,
just the faintest breeze of it, but no sooner had it wafted
by than it would disappear.

That moment, when the doors of the Ark folded upon
the Torah, when the tree of life was closeted for another
week until the next sabbath, that moment reminded

Nicole that life is full of loss. That in the arc of happiness, whatever is the fullest moment is also the moment when it all begins to slip away. Really, her sense of loss had to do not with Torahs or scrolls or putting things away in cabinets, but—just as the liturgy said—with something called the tree of life and reverence for its teachings. The sabbath wasn't really over: it would go on for quite a while, in fact, until an hour after sundown, when three stars would appear in the night sky, even in the thickened sky of Manhattan. Then you would do *havdalah*—with its braided candle, the wine, the *besamim* box full of spices—the ritual that separated the sacred time of the sabbath from the ordinary time of the rest of the week. But when the Torah was returned to the Ark, something was definitely lost, ended. The closing of the Ark meant that the sabbath would inevitably draw to a close for another week, leaving in its wake the prayers and songs and chants, the conversations with friends, wishing them a *shabbat shalom*, a peaceful sabbath. The peace of the sabbath and the community that welcomed it would all too soon disperse into the workaday world of mundane time.

Not that the other six days of the week were lacking in pleasures; far from it. Had David and Nicole been among the throngs of Israelites hastily leaving Egypt, their knapsacks full of unleavened bread, they would also have yearned vociferously for the fleshpots left behind, the lost pomegranates and discos of Cairo. Yet when God appeared in order to lead the Israelites through the wilderness in a pillar of cloud by day and a pillar of fire by night, Nicole and David would have shouldered their belongings, revived their tired children, and forged ahead.

So when the Torah, covered in its velvet mantle, was ritually restored to the Ark until the next shabbat, it was for Nicole the most poignant reminder that eventually on Saturday evening the requisite three stars would come out in the sky, the sabbath reprieve would be over for another week, and ordinary, difficult life would have to be sustained again, amid all of its joys and losses. That the moment of most intense happiness is also the moment at which the fullness of joy begins to fade away.

Craven sentimentality, Nicole would say to herself, utter irrationality. But watching the closing of the Ark, she felt humbled, saddened, almost abased. She would sometimes find herself close to tears.

(on the road)

Nicole was driving car pool one Wednesday afternoon, six children in the back of her Volvo and Caroline sitting next to her on the front seat. The three kids in what they called the "way back" of the station wagon were playing a game together involving complicated hand claps and singing.

> *Miss Lucy has a steamboat*
> *The steamboat has a bell (ding! ding!)*

Miss Lucy went to heaven
The steamboat went to—

Hello, operator.
Please give me number nine
And if you disconnect me
I will chop off your—

Behind the refrigerator
There was a piece of glass—

Nicole could also hear sounds of chomping and snacking, as all the children made a quick feast of a box of Fig Newtons she had passed back to them earlier, and one little boy was showing off by gagging on his cookies, which apparently were too nutritious for his taste. Caroline, next to Nicole, was fiddling with the dial of the radio, listening to one snippet of pop song after another. She finally settled on a song about how life is a hi-i-i-i-ighway, some man was planning to dri-i-ive it all night long. "If you're going my way," he sang, "I want to drive you all night long." If someone tried that with her, Nicole thought, concentrating on her own driving, she wouldn't last too long. That song definitely wasn't meant for her, a mother of two with a day job, daily laundry, a sometime housekeeper, not to mention two rounds of car pool weekly. She glanced at her daughter, wondering what Caroline made of it all.

"My bracket came loose again," Caroline said at the end of the song, turning to Nicole and showing her how her tongue could now fit under the wire of her braces. "At lunch. Maybe because of the corn on the cob."

"Mmmm, I'll call the orthodontist," murmured Nicole, her thoughts elsewhere.

"I got an A on that big Latin test," confided Caroline, "even though I hardly studied a bit. Easy test. Can I go over to Samantha's Saturday night? We're going to rent this video—"

"Great, honey," Nicole answered absently. The boys in the backseat were escalating their own singing. Caroline turned up the radio.

Nicole stopped for a red light and looked around idly, resting her arm on the car door.

Suddenly, across the intersection, she saw Tom, unmistakably Tom, no doubt about it, Tom facing a voluptuous woman in a fire-engine-red dress. The woman had long straight blond hair flowing halfway down her back, and even though her back was to Nicole, Nicole could see that she was furious, shimmering with anger. Red hot with fury. Her hands were on her hips, her shoulders were hunched, and she looked, even from the back, as if she were talking, or maybe shouting, a mile a minute. She would gesture, abruptly, the way someone did in the middle of a brutal quarrel, and she would point accusingly at Tom. Something about Tom, too, looked strange. It took Nicole a few seconds to realize that Tom, of all things, was disheveled. He was leaning in a little too close to the woman, his tie was askew, and he was gripping his cane by its middle and waving it awkwardly in the air, instead of resting it casually on the sidewalk. The woman jabbed the air with her hand. Quickly, in a flash, Tom raised his free hand and slapped her, hard, across the face.

Nicole jumped.

The car behind her honked. The light had changed; what was she doing, just sitting there dreaming? Nicole stepped on the gas. As she passed through the intersection, Tom and the woman were locked in a deep embrace, his free hand tangled in her long blond hair.

"Mrs. Wolfe?" came a voice from the backseat, from the little boy who had been making dramatic gagging noises. "Next time, could you bring Mallomars instead of these yucky Fig Newtons?"

Nicole pulled her car over to the curb and slammed the brakes on so hard that Caroline would have been thrown against the dashboard had she neglected to fasten her seat belt. "If—I—hear—another—word—from you—about a snack," Nicole snarled, turning around on her seat and glaring at the little boy, "you will never—"

(at home)

More and more she was sure it was David who had taken her credit card. And had used it so repeatedly, for such large amounts, that an accountant from MasterCard had finally telephoned Nicole to ask if the sums were legitimate. All the charges were for cash advances—$400 here, $250 there, $600 somewhere else—all within two or three days, but from different banks, apparently to delay suspicion as long as possible. Of course those withdrawals weren't her doing, Nicole told the accountant, panic-stricken; she couldn't possibly have done such a thing. Clearly the card had been stolen. The MasterCard people would look into it to see if they could trace any of the cash advances and the signatures; it was possible that Nicole was actually liable for these loans since she hadn't reported the loss of her card, but meanwhile they would cancel the card so that no one could charge anything else against it. Nicole should know that as of now there would be an investigation and, if they ever discovered the source of the theft, possible criminal charges.

Nicole was desperate. But not at all surprised. There was very little that could surprise her, except maybe David's stupidity, thinking he wouldn't get caught. He must have really needed the money.

When Nicole confronted him that night, he took the high road again. He knew nothing, absolutely nothing. Would he use her credit card? Not he. Why would he do a thing like that?

"Because you always do, you bastard, you've done it before," Nicole told him, infuriated.

"Please," David replied huffily.

He advised her loftily to take her complaints elsewhere, to vent her rage on her friends, that is, her boyfriends. Her *swains*, as David took to calling them, she should vent her fury on her swains. "Bring it up with Jules," David said nastily. Jules probably had complete access to her wallet, maybe every other part of her as well. Then Nicole was even more furious, if that were possible. It was one thing to lie about stealing your wife's credit cards, but it was something else again to implicate all of your wife's friends. David reminded Nicole not to raise her voice quite so much; the children might overhear. Maligned and injured, he retreated into the bathroom, locking the door for good measure behind him.

Nicole waited beside the door for a moment, then darted into Jake's bedroom, where she grabbed a small, brightly colored aluminum chair, the child-size chair from Jake's little worktable. Holding it aloft, she went toward the bathroom, raised the chair over her head, and slammed it as hard as she could against the bathroom door. No sound from the other side of the door; the bathroom might as well have been empty. Again and again Nicole raised the chair and slammed it with all her might against the closed door. She hit the door so hard that large chips of paint came flying off.

When she was finished and took a deep breath, the chair in her hands was mangled, its frame smashed totally out of shape.

(at home)

At dinner a few nights later, David casually mentioned to Nicole that he was a bit short of cash these days, but even so, there was a good movie in the neighborhood, so maybe they could get hold of a baby-sitter that night and go out. Nicole stopped eating and rested her chin in her hands, listening. Jake put a small cube of bread on the end of his fork, aimed it at his sister, and shot, but before

Caroline could retaliate, David glared at both of them and closed his hand over Jake's before another missile could be launched.

Nicole just watched, as if from millions of miles away.

He needed just a little investment in that documentary, explained David, the one she liked so much, about, well, you could say, the *heroism* of teen mothers. The stresses they were under, constantly, from the culture and from within their own peer groups, and how they almost never caved in. Wouldn't, or couldn't, and the toll it took. Just a little more poured into it, David assured everyone, and it's going to be great. It will win all the awards. Daddy will be rich *and* famous, children, won't he.

I'm glad we're all in this together, David said, beaming at the children, his good, dear, darling, and adorable children, light of his life. And their mom, too, star of his firmament. What a family, couldn't be better.

All of us in this together, he repeated. A mom-and-pop operation, David said, just like the good old days. And now, to get his mind off his work, how about that movie?

(the apartment)

I hate him, I just hate him," Nicole sobbed to Tom, shaking with rage and fury and desperation, helplessness and self-pity. Tom could be wonderful then: he would hold her by the shoulders and then bring her very close, cradle her, soothe her, until the anger and crying subsided and Nicole could tell him what had happened. He never said, "That bastard! That son of a bitch!" or anything derogatory at all about David; he even seemed sometimes to be David's advocate in a way that made her angry at Tom but also made her laugh.

"He's cleaned me out again," Nicole moaned. "I'm borderline poverty."

Tom regarded her critically for a moment. "Maybe next you could try chastity and obedience," he said, grinning.

But Tom did urge her to keep her finances totally separate from David's, to keep one bank account in her own name and to deposit her paychecks directly into her own account so that David couldn't just help himself whenever the desire struck him. She could still pay her household bills from that account, but at least it would be secure. And he advised her to change *all* of her credit cards, her charge cards and her telephone credit card, in case David had the urge again to start signing her name to his own bills. Finally he suggested in a mild sort of way that she see a lawyer. And he offered to find her the money for the lawyer if she needed it. After all, he saw lawyers all the time. So she might as well, too. Just a suggestion.

"How come you're so good at this?" Nicole asked suspiciously. "Is it because you're the one with the criminal record? Because you've been fingerprinted?"

"I'm terrible at this," Tom demurred. "I'm not practical enough at all. My friends have always told me I should be more wily, I should be more aggressive, I should make more money. Not to mention my wife." He sighed and

shrugged it off for a moment. "I could do better," he continued. "I could write books, I could do public lectures,
architecture juries. I could go after more projects. That
was part of the reason I lied about that university job—I
thought I *should* go after it. I used to be much better at
keeping myself afloat, you know. In fact, I was a regular
star fucker. You see through me, you know what a charla-
tan I can be. All those country houses I did, in the
Hamptons, in Connecticut. I used to be asked all the time,
after I won those prizes, but I got in the habit of turning
things down. And now I have to deal with lawsuits. *And*
the stories about how I tried to kill my wife. So I'm not
asked anymore. You said it, I remember, the first time we
met: 'From him who hath . . . ' "

"Are you strapped, then?"

"No, not really. You know how I live. On credit, with
Elena. Her money, her foundation, her philanthropy. I
would say that, at the moment, she's not overjoyed with
the situation."

"What does she look like?" Nicole asked casually.
"Elena."

"I've told you—taller than you, dark hair. Pretty."

Nicole hesitated a moment. Then she blurted out,
"Who's the blonde?"

Tom looked startled. "What blonde?" he asked.

"The one in the red dress. You hit her."

Tom suddenly looked furious, as if he might hit
Nicole. She braced herself, but all he said was, "Where
were you?"

"Driving car pool."

Tom was silent, brooding and angry. Finally he said,

very slowly, "My first wife. Her name's Janice. I left her in Richmond when I came north. It was a short marriage."

"Looks like it's not over yet," Nicole ventured caustically.

"She's become a country music singer," Tom continued coldly. "Very successful. Hit records. She was here for a few days to see her agent and her manager. Also, she claims I owe her money. So I shelled out. Under duress, obviously. Anyway, you're the one who keeps telling me nothing is ever really over."

Nicole asked him where he got the money, since he always complained he wasn't making any and had huge insurance and legal bills to pay.

Tom hesitated again. "Elena," he finally said.

"Lucky you," said Nicole. "Isn't there something in your gospels about this? Robbing from the rich to pay the poor?"

"Both my wives are rich," Tom said dryly. "And anyway, that's Robin Hood. Why don't you stick to your own tradition?"

"I'll do that," Nicole said grimly. "It's legalism, remember?"

With the flat of her hand, she slapped Tom across the face as hard as she could. "Who else?" she demanded, her eyes blazing. "Who else don't I know about? How many other marriages? How many other women in fucking red dresses do you kiss in broad daylight?"

Tom was knocked backward with the force of Nicole's blow, but he didn't return the slap or even remonstrate with her. Instead he looked tired and withdrawn.

"I'm at the end of something. I tell you that all the

time," he said quietly. "But that's all I know. That's what the accident was all about. Telling me I can't go any further. And I certainly don't know how to start something new."

Nicole reached out and touched him, gently. She was suddenly deeply in love with him again. "You're exhausted, aren't you."

"I'm sorry—deeply sorry you had to do that," said Tom, rubbing his cheek where she had hit him. "I deserved it."

"Are you so unhappy?" Nicole asked.

"Yes," Tom admitted. "And Janice is the only one. Honestly. I should have told you. It's just . . . well, you know . . . just very hard, sometimes, to unlock yourself."

"No," said Nicole, angry again. "You *liked* smacking her on the street, didn't you. It gave you a thrill, didn't it." Her voice was rising. "You were climbing all over her. And you liked keeping it from me, didn't you. Just for the pleasure of lying about it. One of your benign lies, right? Small potatoes, not damaging at all, right? You—you're a gangster, parading as a saint."

Tom laughed. "Maybe," he agreed. "Takes one to know one, don't you think?" And then he raised his arm in front of his face, in case Nicole should suddenly decide to take another swipe at him.

Nicole didn't apologize, though. She felt perfectly within her rights in exacting her pound of flesh, some equity for Tom's behavior on the street corner. An eye for an eye, it said in her tradition, a slap for a slap. But then, as their anger evaporated, they would make love. Or they would just lie close together on the hard floor or sit side by side, talking companionably and mulling things over.

"Which do you like better," Tom began one day. He was lying on the floor, and Nicole was resting her head on his chest. "Cooked carrots or raw carrots?"

"Raw carrots."

"Raw carrots or broccoli?"

"Oh, broccoli, definitely. How about you?"

"Well, probably raw carrots. Okay, here's another one: Which do you like better, broccoli or cauliflower?"

"Broccoli. You?"

"I hate cauliflower. I wouldn't touch it if my life depended on it. Now, this is getting serious: What's your position on brussels sprouts?"

"I adore them."

"Me, too."

Or sometimes, when she was shredded anyway from the arguing and the tension and the sheer folly of managing her life at home, drained by the children and their endless needs and desires and car pools, tired from the demands of her job, exhausted by trying to maintain some harmony and balance and restraint with David, whose every atom resisted harmony, then Tom could take her roughly, break her apart even more. Sometimes it was just his hands holding her down, implicitly forbidding her to move, sometimes a portentous look, sometimes something more threatening and violent, what she least expected, some almost invisible act of brutality that would leave her choked and gagging. He told her once that he couldn't get her to relax unless he brutalized her in some way. "You *are* a saint," Nicole said warily after one of these episodes. "How terrific."

She rolled over, reaching for her blouse. Managing to get her arms through the sleeves and to fasten a few buttons, Nicole looked blasted but dizzily contented just the same. She stood up unsteadily and careened off toward the bathroom to splash water on her face, to begin to pull herself together.

Tom sat up, fully dressed, and leaned back against the blank wall, watching Nicole intently and buttoning the top button on his shirt so that he could straighten his tie. When he heard the bathroom door close and the sounds of running water, he reached into the pocket of his trousers and took something out. After looking it over for a moment, he quickly found Nicole's handbag where she had dropped it on the floor, extracted her wallet, and slid her credit card back into its accustomed place.

(Sebastian's)

Nicole was sitting at the curving mahogany bar at the entry of Sebastian's, alone. The restaurant was full, but no one else was at the bar, not even the bartender, as if Nicole were sitting in the midst of a cone of solitude. She was sipping a glass of wine and reading. Every now and again she looked up from her book, toward the door, and then back.

to her book. She was restless, anyone could see that, try as she might to appear composed and nonchalant, and even the waiters and maître d' glanced at her with something like apprehension; they knew something was wrong. No one spoke to her, though, as she drank and read and crossed and uncrossed her legs.

The front door to Sebastian's opened suddenly, and Nicole looked up expectantly. But it was only Donna, Tom's assistant, who rushed in, almost hurtling herself toward Nicole. Dressed in the shortest possible leather skirt, tight jacket, and cowboy boots, she looked a little disheveled, as if she'd been running; she was even winded. Nicole was surprised to see her.

Without any preamble whatsoever, Donna told Nicole that Tom was running late, he was held up at a meeting, he wouldn't be there for a while, maybe twenty minutes or so. He had asked Donna to come to Sebastian's and tell Nicole. Realistically it would be more like half an hour. Probably not any longer, but Tokyo was on the line. So Nicole shouldn't expect him any sooner. Sorry.

"Why didn't he just phone?" Nicole asked calmly.

Donna shrugged, as if to say that, in her opinion, a phone call would have done just as well and would have saved her from running all the way over here to this pretentious, pseudo-California restaurant. Although it was also clear that Donna rather relished telling Nicole that she'd have to wait for Tom. That Tom had a full schedule, obligations, meetings, things Donna knew all about and Nicole did not. Donna somehow implied, without saying so, that Tom on this particular day was extremely busy and that it was just a bit difficult for him to squeeze a lunch date into his schedule. In fact, Donna herself was also terribly busy and couldn't stay a moment longer.

"Are you sure," Nicole asked, "that you wouldn't like to stay and have a drink with me while I wait?"

Donna was positive, sorry; she must get right back to the office. Things were hectic; it was just that kind of a day, unbelievable.

The maître d' took all this in, and so did the bartender, who had returned to his post, and so did various waiters floating by in their white jackets and looking on at Nicole with a mixture of amusement and concern. They were no more used to this than Nicole was: Tom had always been prompt, even early, arriving before Nicole and sitting quietly at their table with a book.

"Thank you so much," said Nicole, "for coming over here to tell me. Please tell Tom I'll wait for him at the bar."

After Donna blew out the door, Nicole sat meditatively for a minute or two, leaning against the bar, her finger marking the page in her book where she had stopped reading. Then she closed her book, reached for her hand-bag, and, after a moment's hesitation, drained her glass. She gestured to the bartender, who was busy setting up glasses at the other end of the bar, and asked how much she owed him. The bartender handed her a check, and although she had never paid a bill here before, she did a quick calculation and put some money on the bar. Without waiting for change, she reached for the jacket that the maître d' held out to her. She nodded a quick good-bye to him and left the restaurant.

(outside, a phone booth)

Once outside, Nicole went directly to the nearest phone booth, found her quarter, and made a quick call.

It could have been a business call, it was that methodical. What Nicole said on her end of the telephone was that she *had* been trying to reach him, for ages, why wasn't he ever in his office, and was he possibly free, from now, let's say, until three o'clock? She was downtown right now doing some errands but could meet him in short order.

"I need you to do something for me," Nicole urged into the phone. "To make love to me, okay? No talking, nothing. Just slam me up against a wall—or lay me out on the floor—or fling me up to the ceiling. I mean it, anything you want. Two hours' worth. I want . . . well, I want to get torched, that's all."

After a moment, she laughed. And a moment after that, she looked grim. It was okay, everything was okay.

Nicole hung up and hailed a cab.

(the deli)

Nicole paid the driver and slid out of the cab in front of a deli on the corner of Broadway. She went right in and up to the counter.

"Two coffees," she said. "To go. One regular and one black. Sweet'n Low on the side." Then she added, "I'll pick them up in a moment."

There was a ladies' room in a small corridor at the back of the deli, not a large one and not a very clean one, either. Nicole entered a stall, locked the door, and then simply rolled off her panty hose, slipping first one bare foot and then the other back into her leather pumps. She stowed her panty hose, neatly folded, in her pocketbook.

A paper bag was waiting for her on the counter as she came out of the bathroom. Nicole picked it up and paid her bill.

(the Wolfes' bedroom)

Nicole was lying in bed, propped up on her pillows and reading *The New York Times.* A cup of coffee was on the night table beside her, the coffee was steaming, and every now and again Nicole would take a sip. She was in the middle of the Obituaries page, which she read first thing each morning, top to bottom, small print included. She had to know who had died and, more than that, who the deceased were: the names of the surviving spouse, the grieving children, grandchildren, and beloved nieces and nephews, who was mourning them, what church or synagogue they belonged to, what Sisterhood they were president of, what charities they supported, what disease they died of, and which funeral home would handle the burial. Nicole's theory, born of long reading, was that people died in droves, by profession. There would be a run on dead surgeons, let's say, followed soon after by a run on dead screenwriters or labor leaders or abstract painters.

As she read, the telephone rang. One ring. Nicole finished the column she was reading, folded the paper, and dialed a number. "Did you ring me?" she asked Tom when he answered right away. "Aren't you at work kind of early?"

Tom was just checking in. He hadn't heard her voice yet this morning and it was already eight-thirty; he had just wanted to say hello and to tell her that he'd gotten an early start this morning, for a change, had left the house, picked up coffee, and gotten in to his studio even before his assistant. Nicole told him about that morning's obits: today it was electrical engineers, and the odds-on favored names for grandchildren were Jessica and Zachary, with Emma and the apparently unisex Jesse well placed for the future.

"Where are you?" Tom asked. "Exactly."

"In bed. Lying in bed. Sometimes after David and the kids leave, I go back to bed for a while, to catch my breath for the day."

"What are you wearing?"

Nicole told him that she was still wearing what she had slept in, a loose, faded pink T-shirt and underpants. Earlier, when she had gotten breakfast for everyone and had sent them off for the day to their various destinies of school and work, she had pulled on a pair of dungarees. But now she was back in what she had slept in, to have this little luxury of morning coffee in bed. She would have to get dressed soon and get going; she didn't have to teach her classes today but had errands to do, a lot of paper grading, and a faculty meeting at noon. Would they meet for lunch? She thought she could get free by one.

"Tell me what position you're in," Tom demanded. "On your back?"

"Yes, lying on my back. My knees are up. The paper's propped on my knees," Nicole answered obediently.

Now Tom had a new sort of demand. "Put your hand between your legs, please."

"Tom," Nicole demurred, "if we're going to do this, wait a second. I want to make sure the front door is locked. Just a sec. I'm going to put you on hold." Before Tom could object, Nicole pushed a button on her phone, rolled her eyes, and climbed out of bed. So much for a quiet cup of coffee.

Instead of going to the front door to check the lock, however, Nicole slid back into her jeans and slipped her bare feet into a pair of old penny loafers. She went into the kitchen and took a large pile of laundry out of the dryer. Quickly she dumped the clean laundry on the kitchen table. Then she picked up the kitchen phone. "Okay, Tom," she breathed into it, "I'm back. You were saying?"

"In bed? Lying down again? On your back?"

"Well, on my side, really, talking to you," answered Nicole, standing at the kitchen table with the receiver cradled on her shoulder. She began to sort the laundry. David's clothes in one pile, Jake's in another, Caroline's in a third, and so forth. Towels in a separate pile. Socks in a separate pile. Napkins. Dish towels. "But I locked the door. Unless you want the super walking in."

"Lie on your back, please, the way you were before. With your knees up."

"Okay," Nicole said softly, shaking out one of Jake's T-shirts and folding it. She picked up another shirt, this time one of David's.

"Now, touch yourself, please."

"Umm, Tom, if I start this . . ." Caroline's nightgown was next, and then Nicole rummaged through the pile to find matching tops and bottoms for two sets of Jake's pajamas. Then a few of her own bras and panties.

"Touch yourself. Very slowly. Lightly. You can hardly feel it."

"Tom," said Nicole, very slowly, "look, um, you're asking me . . . " and she paused, as if trying to collect her thoughts. She picked up another T-shirt. Every now and again she breathed audibly into the phone.

"A little faster," Tom directed.

"It . . . is . . . fast," Nicole said thickly, waiting a few moments while she smoothed out some napkins. "I can't help it. It's . . . um . . . uh . . . fast. What you said. . . ." By this time she was folding more quickly, Jake's shirts, David's underpants, dish towels, whatever was in reach. She folded neatly and quickly, stacking up the folded clothes in their right piles. When she got to the large bath towels, she had to lean back to shake them out and match the edges, cradling the phone carefully on her shoulder so that it wouldn't drop. There were long silences, which Nicole punctuated with a sudden sharp intake of breath or an occasional low moan. "Oh, God," she moaned softly at one point, "oh, God."

"Keep going," Tom said, "don't stop." The laundry was stacking up nicely.

With the last towel folded and only the socks left to do, Nicole decided it was time to come.

(at home)

Caroline seemed to be coming down with the flu, Nicole thought. The child dragged herself around, played with her food at meals, and procrastinated endlessly with her homework. She was even listless about telephone calls. Instead of the long, elaborate conversations she normally had—sitting thronelike in the middle of her bed with her homework spread around her, along with a few teen magazines, a bag of Pepperidge Farm cookies, and usually some nail polish, hand cream, or a razor in case she was moved to hold the receiver in one hand and her beauty preparations in the other—she now simply answered the phone and hung up soon after.

She had circles under her eyes and snapped at Jake even more than usual. After a few days of this moodiness, Nicole began to worry and would press the inside of her wrist to Caroline's forehead every time she got the chance, much to Caroline's irritation. But clearly Caroline had no fever and nothing was hurting her, or so she said.

"What is it, then?" asked her mother, sitting one afternoon on the side of Caroline's bed while Caroline lay on her back, reading or pretending to read a book of Arthurian legends. "You've seemed awfully tired lately," Nicole continued. "Are you sure something isn't hurting you? Your throat? Your ears?" Nicole thought she should call the pediatrician anyway. Anemia? Mono? Were her braces bothering her? Did she not get an invitation to someone's birthday party?

Caroline shook her head.

"What *is* it?" Nicole asked desperately. "What's the matter?"

Putting her open book over her face, Caroline lay still for a moment and then suddenly burst into tears. "The letter," she blurted out, "the letter."

"What letter?" asked Nicole, completely puzzled.

"On your desk," Caroline choked. "With no name on it, but it said 'Dear Nicole.'" She removed the book from across her face and glared at her mother, still crying.

"What are you talking about?" asked Nicole. "I don't know what you're talking about."

Caroline suddenly turned on her in a fury. "You know perfectly well what I'm talking about," she choked out through her tears. "I saw that letter. I know what that letter means. From some man. It says you have sex. That he loves to have sex with you. That he wants to keep doing it. And all those disgusting words for it! I can't believe you

get letters like that!" She put the book back over her face
and lost herself in a fury of weeping.

Dear Nicole, the letter had said, *I want more than anything else to skewer you—back and front, front and back,
around and around—and skewer you again so thoroughly
you will vomit stars. You will forget everything you ever
knew, babble in tongues from the back of your throat, flame
out mystical numbers like the Zohar. You will have wings of
fire, you will ride a chariot into the heavens.*

*When I am around you, I am possessed by a demon,
and will pound and pulverize you into molecules until you
blaze and writhe at nothing more than a touch, a look.
You will strip off your clothes and dance before the Ark of
my desire. . . .*

"That wasn't a letter," said Nicole, taking Caroline,
big as she was, into her arms and holding tightly as the
girl sobbed. "I know you thought it was a letter, but it
wasn't."

"What was it, then?"

"I know it looked like a letter," said Nicole in a quiet
voice and speaking very slowly so that Caroline could listen to every word. "But it's fiction, or, really, *midrash,*
which means storybook interpretations of the Bible."

"I don't get it," said Caroline. "Didn't some man write
it? And why did it say 'Dear Nicole'?"

"Yes, someone wrote it," Nicole assured her. "One of
my students. In my Bible class. He wants to write stories
based on the Bible; he tries to write *midrash.* He wrote it,
and sent it to me, so that I could read it and make sugges-

tions for him. Help him with it. Like I do with my other students."

"I don't believe you," Caroline said baldly. "I think you're lying. I think you and this guy are having sex."

"You don't have to believe me," said her mother in the same even tone, "but it's true. We are not having sex. But I *am* helping him with his writing. Do you think if it were a real letter about my having sex with him that I would leave it out on my desk?"

"I think you forgot," Caroline said judiciously. "I think you made a mistake and forgot to hide it. I bet you have more letters like that, hidden somewhere, all about having sex."

"No," insisted Nicole, "I don't. And I don't expect you to understand what you read, either. There were a lot of words and meanings there, from the Bible, that you don't understand yet. It wasn't really written for a child. Even for a child as grown-up as you."

"I still think you're lying," said Caroline, suspicious but not crying anymore.

"That's okay," Nicole said. "I'm not lying. I have sex only with Daddy. But now I understand why you've seemed so tired lately. I'm very proud of you for finally telling me about that *midrash* you found. You're a brave and wonderful girl. Now we'll both feel better." Nicole kissed her. "And you don't have to keep it a secret," she said, continuing to kiss and cuddle her daughter, who was finally allowing her mother to hold her. "It's not a secret that I help my students with their writing. You can talk about it, and you can ask me about it again, okay?"

"I still don't believe you," Caroline said flatly.

(at home)

The next morning, after David had gone to work and the kids had been picked up for school, Nicole climbed up on a chair and unhooked each of the smoke detectors from the walls of her apartment, pocketing the batteries. Then she went into her bedroom, opened the bottom drawer of her dresser, and from underneath a pile of sweaters she pulled out a packet of paper. The packet was slender, hardly a packet at all but held together with several rubber bands. After removing the rubber bands, Nicole read over the few sheets of paper, impassively, barely blinking. It could have been bills she was looking at or a stack of recipes, something you would look at carefully but certainly not linger over. Then she went into the kitchen, found a book of matches, and, one by one, burned each piece of paper in the sink.

(the Wolfes' bedroom, dawn)

David rolled over to the edge of the double bed and picked up the alarm clock on the bedside table. Bringing it right up to his nose because his reading glasses were still on the table, he squinted, then turned the clock around slightly and squinted again. He yawned, stretched, glanced over at Nicole, who was still fast asleep, way over on her edge of the bed, her back to her husband. David gave his sleeping wife a moment's thought and then inched toward her, under the covers, until he was close enough to her body to reach it with ease. Nicole still slept soundly. David tentatively put his hand on her thigh, stroking it lightly.

Nicole didn't react. After a few moments of running his hand lightly up and down her thigh, David moved his hand upward and felt inside her underpants. He continued to stroke her lightly with his fingers, her buttocks, her legs, whatever he could touch easily, playing with her, searching for her in the midst of her drowsiness. Nicole finally moaned—or maybe just grunted—in her sleep, a long, low, throaty sound that meant she was waking up, but not too quickly. She shifted a little under the covers so that David could reach her more easily.

When David had his wife's body rocking gently the way he wanted it to, even though Nicole's eyes were still closed, he quickly lowered her underpants to her ankles and rolled on top of her. She sleepily helped David along, kicking off her panties, but she still didn't open her eyes.

"What time is it?" she finally murmured.

"Shhh," David whispered. "It's early, we've got time." Then, a moment later, he added, "Do we need to use anything?" Nicole shook her head. David guided himself inside her.

"Someone's . . . got to . . . make lunch for Jacob," Nicole brought out sleepily. "His class is going to the Planetarium . . . the ozone layer."

"Shhh," repeated David, pulling up Nicole's T-shirt and putting his mouth to her chest. He caressed her a little with his tongue, kissed her shoulders, her neck, behind her ear. "I'll do it, don't worry," he whispered, moving slowly up and down.

Nicole let out a long sigh of assent.

David picked up Nicole's limp arm to check the time on her wristwatch and then got to work in earnest. Nicole smiled at him drowsily, allowing herself to move with him as he rocked rhythmically back and forth. Then, quickly, she locked her arms around him, holding him to her as tightly as she could. Suddenly David heaved and crashed, collapsing over his wife with all the force and grace of a tree felled in a forest. When he came to, Nicole was kissing his neck. He picked up her wrist a second time, checked her watch, and collapsed on top of his wife once again.

There was a knock at the bedroom door, the kind of knock produced by a small fist, insistent. David hurriedly rolled off of Nicole, groaning in annoyance.

"Mom! Dad!" came a voice from the other side of the door. "Wake up—I have a school trip today—"

"Back to bed, Jake," his father ordered, getting the words out with some difficulty. "Too early."

"We'll all get up in a few minutes," added Nicole.

"—to the Planetarium . . . and I need—" continued Jacob, punctuating his needs with a few more poundings at the door.

"I know, I know," Nicole interrupted. "Don't worry."

"Go back to bed," David ordered again. "Mommy will take care of it. I promise." He put his arms around his wife and held her very tightly for a minute, and then he held her more loosely, breathing into her hair while they both drifted back into sleep again, until the alarm went off.

(Sebastian's)

It wasn't that Tom was appalled, or even angry. In fact, he listened with an air of studious sobriety throughout most of Nicole's recitation, leaning judiciously back in his chair. At one point he had cleared his throat as if he were a lawyer getting to the troublesome part of a deposition, but then, as Nicole went on with her story, he seemed wryly amused and even burst out laughing when she told him how the man had asked, as he had helped her on with her jacket and ushered her to the door, why she had *really* called him out of the blue and when he could expect another summons. Then he called over the waiter to ask if he could borrow a cigarette. "Just one," Tom explained, "I've stopped smoking." But the waiter apologetically turned him down flat, reminding him that smoking in a restaurant like Sebastian's was now prohibited, against the law, so Tom murmured something like "Oh, yes, of course, hmm . . . " and asked for the check instead, drumming his fingers on the table. As he fumbled with his credit card, Nicole said she had to go to the bathroom, please excuse her, and Tom politely rose half out of his chair, as he always did, when Nicole stood up and left the table to go down-stairs.

As she came out of the stall, however, she was startled to see Tom right there, in the ladies' room, leaning against the door so that no one else could enter. He looked coldly murderous. Nicole decided instantly that it was best to treat his entry as an ordinary matter, so she bent over the sink to wash her hands, all the while watching him in the mirror as he locked the door behind him. When she was finished she started for the door, but Tom blocked it, re-fusing to move. Nicole hesitated, getting a little angry her-self. "Excuse me—" she said, expecting him to step aside. Enough was enough. Instead he grabbed her by the shoul-ders and shoved her against the wall.

"Don't you ever—" he began furiously.

"Then don't *you* stand me up."

Holding her tight against the wall with his left hand, Tom raised his right arm and swung. At the last second, though, he somehow caught himself and stopped, just a fraction short of her cheek. Nicole flinched.

Tom abruptly let go of her and backed off, his eyes tightly shut, breathing hard, almost shuddering. "Look what you've turned me into," he whispered hoarsely, "a psychopath, violent, deranged—" He opened and clenched his fists, barely restraining himself.

"Go ahead," Nicole taunted him. "Let's see if you can get it up this time!"

Now Tom grabbed her again, hard, shoving her back against the wall so violently that her head banged against it. "I am going to ram you," he threatened, jamming his pelvis against hers. "This time you're going to get it." But instead of ripping into her, he took her head in both hands and thrust his tongue inside her mouth, so deep and so hard that she gagged. Tears came to her eyes. But he wouldn't let her go.

Someone rattled the doorknob. Finally he released her. Choking and gasping for air, Nicole wiped her eyes and wiped the back of her hand against her mouth. When the doorknob rattled again, Tom, looking exceedingly pleased with himself, opened it and held it with great aplomb as a startled woman entered, glaring at Nicole and Tom as if they were criminals. Nicole stumbled out, still wiping her eyes and trying to catch her breath. When they reached the main level of the restaurant, Tom quietly pressed a twenty-dollar bill into the hand of the maître d', retrieved Nicole's jacket from the coat check, and courteously helped her on with it.

Once out the door, they started off down the street as if total strangers, keeping their distance from each other. Tom seemed to be paying no attention to her; his hands were shoved deep in his pockets as if he were afraid that, unrestrained, he might take another swing at her. From the corner of her eye, Nicole saw him shake his head. She reached for him. "I'm sorry," she began, "I shouldn't have—"

Tom shook her off. But a second later he turned toward her. "If you ever—" he began roughly, but suddenly softened. Instead of finishing his thought, he enveloped her in his arms.

"Do you love me?" she asked. Tom held her and didn't answer.

(the campus)

Jules and Nicole pushed their chairs back and left the meeting with a small group of their colleagues, all of whom seemed to be talking at once.

"Two-thirds of the 'Great Books' reading list still privileges the status quo, or worse," a woman was saying angrily to her colleagues. "All we're doing with Homer is empowering militarism and male bonding—"

"You can't get rid of *The Iliad*," another colleague, a man, interrupted. "We'd all lose our jobs, for one thing."

Jules stopped dead in his tracks, folded his arms across his chest, closed his eyes, and began to sway back and forth. "Forgive us, O Lord," he began, rhythmically rocking back onto his heels, "forgive us our manifold sins. We teach *The Iliad*. We teach sexism, racism, ageism, obese-ism. We have published rather than perished. We have renovated our apartments. . . . " With his eyes closed, Jules was rocking faster and faster.

"Get a life, Jules," the woman said, still furious. She slipped her arm through Nicole's. "Squarely in the rear guard, as usual," she said, gesturing toward Jules, who was lumbering beside her, still swaying and mumbling to himself like a caricature of an old man at prayer. "Lunch?" she asked Nicole, and then, without waiting for an answer, "A multiculturalist agenda would at least liberate us from retro-creeps like—"

"I'd love to," interrupted Nicole, disengaging herself and checking her watch, "but I have to go. Bye, everyone." She waved briefly to no one in particular. Jules followed her outside.

"Busy lady, aren't you," he said once he and Nicole were both out on the campus, walking toward the main gates. "No one has to tell *you* to get a life, right?"

"Knock it off, Jules," Nicole said. "It's only a lunch date. And I have to pick up some Seldane for David's hay fever before I forget. Oh—I'd better make sure I have the prescription." She leaned back against a tree and began rummaging in her handbag, finding a bunch of laundry tickets as well as coupons for things like shampoo and Q-Tips. Caroline was obsessed with finding the perfect conditioner, not to mention the perfect liquid soap, deodorant, and self-tanning cream.

"Of course, of course," replied Jules. When Nicole didn't answer—she had found the prescription and was taking out a small mirror and her lipstick to make a quick check—Jules continued. "I'm very happy for you," he said.

Nicole looked up, surprised.

"You've finally found someone who's a match for you," Jules went on. "Someone you can give yourself totally to. Don't forget, I know you. I know who you are. But be careful. You could really fuck it up."

"What do you mean, be careful?" Nicole asked, putting back her lipstick and mirror and slipping the items for a pharmacy visit into her jacket pocket. "I'm always careful. I don't know what you're talking about."

"Oh, yes, you do," he replied.

Nicole didn't answer. She actually hadn't been listening to much of anything for the last half hour or so. Her mind was on Tom, on meeting him in just a short while at the apartment, where they would share their tuna salad sandwiches and savage or soothe each other, depending on how the day had gone for each of them. The apartment key was in her jacket pocket as well; she had been fingering it all during the faculty meeting and once had even pressed the sharp tip of it so hard into her thumb that she had lost her breath for a second and had to close her eyes. But of course her colleagues hadn't noticed, so intent were they on reformulating the canon and then getting on to lunch. Now she would get on to lunch, too. But she would have to shake Jules.

"You've never been careful in your life," Jules went on. He suddenly sounded very angry, very definitive. "Never. You are profligate."

Nicole shoved herself away from the tree she had been leaning against and started walking, Jules right at her side.

"What are *you* so angry about?" she asked, getting the pace up to a fast clip.

"You. How dangerous you are—"

"Not to you."

"To yourself, wiseass," Jules continued hotly. "I know about those calls you get at public phone booths. Those so-called lunch dates. And, don't forget, I know about the apartment. 'Utterly empty,' right? Look, I'm just trying to protect you. Because I know that you'll jeopardize everything."

"Thanks so much."

"All I'm telling you," he said with great intensity, "is to be careful. You love him. You've finally met someone you really, truly love. Probably for the first time in your life—"

"Jules, please," Nicole interrupted, stepping into the street and putting out her arm to flag down a cab. "If you're so worried about my well-being, why don't you come over tonight and cook dinner?"

"—and you've handed him everything on a tray," Jules continued, ignoring her interruption. "You're ready to give him anything. You're naked for someone—finally. But you are profligate. You will risk everything. So just please be careful. Don't lose him. I care too much about you to let you lose Tom the way I've seen you lose everyone else. Be careful, I'm telling you. Don't fuck things up."

"Can't you give it a rest?" Nicole asked angrily as a taxi slowed down next to her.

"That's what I mean," said Jules, stepping back and not even thinking to open the car door for Nicole. "What you want is for Tom never to be able to walk away from you. The stakes are too high this time. So don't fuck things up. Again."

Nicole opened the door to the taxi. But then she paused for a moment. Something had just occurred to her. "Do you still love me, Jules?" she asked, turning to face him directly.

"I told you once," Jules answered, suddenly serious and reflective, even though they were both standing in the middle of the street, "love isn't everything. You know that."

If Nicole hadn't been rushing off to lunch, if she had had the time to talk to Jules then, she might have told him that, yes, she agreed, love wasn't everything. Jules was

right, quite clearly. Maybe that's why she sometimes felt
so unsteady, so shaky, with Tom, even though he was
promising to love her always and forever, love her with his
dying breath, because, really, she'd known all along that
love wasn't everything. The more Tom promised and
swore and dithered on about how he would love her
forever—*forever*, he would say in a dark, incantatory
whisper—the more insubstantial he seemed. Once, at
Sebastian's, Tom had taken a hundred-dollar bill from his
wallet, rolled it into a cone, and set it aflame at the table,
as if fireworks were a sign of his covenant of love. *To my
last breath*, he had repeated while Nicole had waited for
the smoke alarms to go off and the waiters to rush over
and thrust the two of them out of the restaurant. But nothing had happened; the hundred-dollar bill had quickly
burned itself out on a china saucer, and Tom had doused
the embers with some water from his glass. Afterward,
hours later, Nicole had wondered if a genuine, used hundred-dollar bill would burn quite so quickly or whether
the bill might, just might, have been counterfeit. And who
carried around one-hundred-dollar bills, anyway? She
was ashamed of herself for doubting Tom, whom she
loved inordinately. But was that supposed to be love?

Unfortunately she sometimes thought it was.
Sometimes Nicole thought she'd made a terrible mistake,
an unforgivable one, believing that because she loved
someone, or someone loved her, there might be a fraction
of change in the laws of the universe, a tiny sliver of belief,
something to hold on to. But she knew Jules was right.
Love wasn't everything.

Nicole slid into the taxi and drove off to meet Tom.

Gangsters

(a long time ago, in the kitchen)

Is it worth it?" Jules had asked her once, a long time ago.

Nicole hadn't answered. There was silence, total silence. What could she say?

"Is it?" Jules had urged again. They had been sitting at Nicole's kitchen table, drinking coffee, a Bible open in front of each of them as they made notes on what they would teach that week in their "Great Books" course.

Nicole finally looked him straight in the eye. "Probably," she answered sullenly. "I guess I'd have to say yes."

"That's good," Jules said smugly, with great satisfaction, as if knowing she could not possibly have answered otherwise. "Hold out your hand," he ordered.

Nicole put down her coffee cup and stretched her arm out in front of her, toward Jules.

"If it's so worth it," he continued, studying her hand, "then why is your hand shaking?"

"Got me," Nicole said darkly. "Caffeine?"

"Hold still," he ordered again. "Stop acting as if I'm killing you. It's worth it for me, too. You're terrific fun, did I ever tell you that? You really are."

"That sounds to me an awful lot like good-bye," Nicole retorted angrily. "Terrific fun? Good Lord."

Jules continued to study her hand until she withdrew it.

"What are you so angry at?" Nicole finally asked, picking up her coffee cup and making sure that her hand

(187)

wouldn't shake. It seemed to her that she was always asking Jules that question. What *was* he always so angry
about?

"You," Jules burst out, "just you. You jeopardize
everything. You don't care what you ruin. You're like an
avalanche—you destroy everything in your path. You
can't even do what I counted on you for."

What was that? Nicole had asked him, curious despite
her anger and fear. What had he counted on her for?

"To pull me out of my marriage," Jules admitted
glumly. "You couldn't even do that."

Nicole was amazed. Of course she couldn't do that.
Whatever had made Jules think she could? If she had tried
to spring him from his marriage to Martha, she would
have had to blow up her own marriage. And the truth was,
she *liked* her marriage; it suited her, despite the chaos and
brutishness that was all too often her daily fare. David was
a fine man, really, staunchly loyal to his family, a good father, an engaging companion, and certainly not humdrum
or tedious, whatever his flaws. At least she knew that her
marriage would never evaporate, like so many others, out
of terminal boredom.

Moreover David pretty much left her alone, to her own
devices, devious as they might be, despite all the bombast
and neutron bombs he impetuously hurled around at
home. He actually, appearances to the contrary, did not
intrude upon her. That was the private, unspoken pact she
had made with David: she would get to live her own life,
do as she wished, maintain her secret cycle of friendships
and intimacy, and in return, she would put up with the
chaos of David's enthusiasms and angers, the times when

he would wreak havoc and play the ringmaster, all more or less simultaneously. Whatever trepidation Nicole felt was mitigated, softened, by the price David exacted from her, by his scattershot brutality and violence; it was her ransom. You do as you wish, you live as an outlaw for love—or something that looks like love—you pay the price, which is reasonable and just. There was even a certain elegance to the bargain. Nicole had long ago given it her tacit consent. Not to mention the small, private matter of how tender and sweet it felt to have David's hand resting companionably under her body at night while she slept.

Deep down, though, Nicole didn't believe in divorce, not really, and certainly not for her. Marriage is a sacrament, thought Nicole—even if you don't believe in God, it is a holy vow, irretrievable. Craven sentimentality, she would think, but, nevertheless, she knew no other way to describe it. There was something about her marriage to David—beyond the children they shared, beyond the random intimacy, beyond the touch of David's hand under her back at night when she slept turned away from him— that could not, should not, be torn asunder.

But although Nicole was perfectly willing to call marriage a sacrament, sacred and indelible, she knew that murder and mayhem were also part of the deal, an additional clause, an addendum, as it were. When God in Genesis created Adam and Eve, he created marriage as well, in the very next sentence—a man should leave his father and mother and cleave to his wife, so that they become one flesh. Never mind that right away there are two kids murdering each other. In Genesis as in Manhattan:

there is marriage, and soon there are children and bills and orthodontia and soccer practice and murder; it happens in every family.

Yet that was no reason to jettison the marriage, Nicole thought, although walking away was obviously tempting. So she really, truly, had no intention of trading in her marriage with David to run off with someone, no matter how much she yearned for those lustrous moments and hours of abandon, and certainly she was not about to run off with Jules, who was decidedly losing his tarnish. She'd rather redecorate her living room. She'd rather . . . she'd rather have a new kitchen, which she badly needed, and maybe even partition off a small part of it to make a laundry room. She mentioned these possible renovations to Jules. After all, he had just been made a dean at the university, his paycheck was just that much more generous, so he and Martha were undertaking a long overdue renovation of their apartment. Certainly he must know of an available contractor? How about a decorator, just in case?

"That's why this is over," Jules said, furious. "I'm out of here. Otherwise, I'll string you along forever. And I'd end up pushing you over a cliff. Not a bad idea, is it? I'll shove you over a cliff and watch your body bounce from rock to rock."

"Do you love me?" Nicole asked, knowing in advance what the answer would be but helpless not to ask anyway. It was one thing to be loyal to David, to somehow maintain the camaraderie and intimacy of her marriage no matter what, but quite another to be told that she was about to face a devastating loss.

So she would have to listen while Jules told her that

her hand was shaking and she had better stop it, she had better get herself under control. When she was in a better mood, Jules would say, she really was a lot of fun.

Jules stared at her intently. "Stand up," he said.

"Why?"

"Because you really are getting thinner," he answered solicitously. "I want to look at you and see what's happening to you."

"You know what it is," Nicole said sullenly, pushing her chair out and getting up. "I get a little jumped by all this. Big deal."

"Stand up," he said.

Nicole stood up and so did Jules.

He pushed her shoulders to the wall and backed a few steps away from her. "Pull up your blouse," he ordered, and when Nicole hesitated, he added harshly, "Don't think I want to see your breasts, just your middle."

Nicole pulled up her blouse, to just below her breasts. Jules looked at her for a moment but didn't touch her or reach out to her. She pulled her blouse as tightly as she could across her breasts. She seemed numb or paralyzed; she hardly moved.

Jules pinched her waist roughly. "Look at this," he said, holding on to a wedge of her skin. "Thin, but flabby. Getting out of shape."

"Are you going to make love to me?" Nicole asked.

"No," Jules said, "absolutely not. One fuck and I'll be hooked again. Like eating one potato chip. But you're worse, you're like taking a drug, you're lethal. Cigarettes, coke. I've been mainlining you. I've got track marks up and down my arm. But I'm kicking the habit."

And I'm lying to you, Nicole thought. It's not worth it. Nothing is worth this.

(at home)

The Wolfe family was at dinner, all four of them, eating comfortably at their table in the kitchen. David served the meal for a change, bringing it over from the stove and helping the two children first, while Nicole leaned across the table to Jake and cut his meat into small pieces. Then she and David finally addressed their own meals, nodding to each other over their glasses of wine but soon absorbed by their children's conversation. Caroline was explaining that her English class at Thackeray was studying the Ten Commandments and she had to memorize them for tomorrow. She started to recite them while Jake tried to persuade his father that what the family really needed was a dog, and that he, Jacob Wolfe, six years old, would happily walk the dog several times a day and even late at night, even though it would be past his bedtime.

David, meanwhile, was telling Nicole that his meeting with the promotional people went really well, the script looked great, and now it was just a matter of getting the whole deal green-lighted, which should be, keep your fingers crossed, pro forma. Nicole looked tired and didn't eat much.

"Caroline first," she said finally, "and then Jake, and

then Daddy. We can't listen to everyone at once. This is supposed to be polite dinner table conversation." But no one paid the slightest attention, and all three of them kept talking. Caroline was running down the Commandments, one by one, memorizing.

"What's adultery?" Jake asked.

"When someone who is married has sex with someone else, not the person they're married to," Nicole answered almost without thinking.

Caroline laughed. "You know what Marisa said in school today?"

"What."

"Mrs. Trowbridge asked who knows what 'Thou shalt not commit adultery' means, and Marisa said"—here Caroline was overcome with the giggles—"Marisa said, 'Does that mean you're not allowed to grow up?'"

The whole family laughed, and Caroline continued, "But I get what adultery is. It's like you and that guy," she said, turning to her mother.

Nicole, in sudden alarm, studied her daughter.

"Yes," Caroline said decisively, "adultery is what happens with you and your student. What he wrote in that letter."

Everyone was suddenly silent.

"That letter?" asked David, leaning across the table and staring intently at Caroline. "What letter?"

"The letter I found," Caroline began to explain patiently, "that says that Mommy and some man are having an adultery. That he wants to have it with her again and again. The one that Mommy says is fiction." She turned to Nicole. "What did you call it, Mom? That other word?"

More silence.

Jake was the first to say something. "When you and Dad get divorced," he asked Nicole, "could I get a dog?"

David slammed his fist on the table, and everyone was silent again. "Fiction," he said at last, mulling over the word and still speaking directly to Caroline. "Mommy says it's fiction, does she?"

"*Midrash!*" announced Caroline triumphantly. "Now I remember!"

Caroline suddenly noticed that both of her parents were staring at her with great intensity and that her mother hadn't said a word. "You *told* me I could talk about it," she shouted at Nicole. "You *said* it wasn't a secret. I *knew* I shouldn't have said anything. I *knew* you were a liar." With that, she bolted from the table and ran out of the kitchen. A moment later a door slammed.

"*Midrash,*" murmured David, leaning back in his chair and studying Nicole. "That's inventive. Even for you."

(the apartment, midnight)

I don't know what I'm doing here. In this apartment. In the middle of the night. I can't believe I'm doing this. Tell me, what is it about me making me do this? Just tell me.

All I know is, I lie. I had to lie to get here, and I'll have to lie tomorrow morning when I get home. And I can't lie, I'm no good at lying. But I lie all the time, it's horrible. Even to my own children—even to my sweet, pure, beautiful daughter who probably will never trust me again. And she would be right, that's the horrible thing. I can't believe what I say: Oh, by the way, I have a conference next week, upstate. I'll be gone Tuesday night. Here's the number, in an emergency. I can't believe I say those things. How can I do it? And not once, but time after time? What has happened to me?"

"You can go home, you know."

"I'm not going home. Don't be ridiculous. Good Lord."

"You can, it's all right. I'll be here for you, I'll wait for you."

"Sure. Thanks. I can go home."

"Really, it's all right. It's not far, and your car's right outside."

"Why is it so all right with you? Why should I go home, why? Do you want me to go home, is that it? The first time we can spend the night together and now you don't want to go through with it?"

"I want you to do whatever you want to do. Whatever you're comfortable with—"

"Comfortable! What are you talking about? Does this look to you like comfortable? Here I am, cooped up with you—everyone thinks I'm at some conference—and you—"

"—because I know you'll turn around and come back."

Tom poured them both some more wine. Nicole shouldn't have, she knew, but she downed some anyway.

"I will, won't I. I'll just turn right around. I'll spend the whole night on the road, won't I. Just going back and forth. I'll get killed on the road. You know I'm too drunk to drive. Why do you want to put me in a car? So I'll get killed, is that it?"

"I'll drive you. It will be okay. I'll drive you home."

"No, you won't. You're as drunk as I am. Do you think I'd get into a car with you? Are you crazy? Isn't it enough that I'm back in this apartment with you, in the middle of the night—I have to drive around all night with you, too? How can I even think these things! How can you, of all people? What about your sainthood? What about your wife? What are *you* doing here? No matter what you say, your life is fine without me. In fact, I can't figure out what you'd want me for at all. So why are you here? And besides—"

"You know why. You know why I'm here."

"And besides, what the hell am I doing here next to you? It's not even about sex, for God's sake. If it were about sex, maybe being here would make some sense. I'm sorry. I can't explain this. All I know is I can't stay."

"Then you'll have to go. . . ."

"I can't go, don't you see? Do you think my going solves anything? I can't even go, that's the horrible thing. I have to stay. I'm sorry, I'm terribly sorry. I shouldn't be saying these things to you—"

"Yes, you should, if—"

"No, I shouldn't. I'm not trying to hurt you, really I'm

not. I just can't bear what I'm doing. And I can't stop, either."

"You're not hurting me. Really."

"Oh, please. I'm hurting everyone. You. Myself. I can't even think what I'm doing to my children. Especially my children. What I said to Caroline about that stupid, obscene letter—I can't believe it! And hurting them means hurting myself. I love you, don't you see that? I love you, and it's a catastrophe—I'm all at odds with myself, can't you see? I'm hurting my kids, and I'm hurting you, and I'm hurting myself—"

"No, no, you aren't hurting me. Listen, just listen for a minute—"

"I can't, I'm sorry. I just can't stop. Something happened. I can't stop, there's something in me that won't stop—"

"You're giving me a great gift. You know that, don't you, what a gift this is? If it were me deeply, deeply upset—and crying—you'd think it was a gift, wouldn't you?"

"Yes. Of course. I know that. But what I'm giving you now doesn't feel like a gift. Not to me. It just feels like a mess. It feels like confusion. Panic."

He tried to put his arm around her, but she shook him off. After that, he didn't try again. She would just have to keep going.

"It feels like Tisha B'Av. Do you know what Tisha B'Av is? No, of course you don't. How could you? It's a Jewish holiday, in the middle of the summer. Tisha B'Av means 'the Ninth of Av,' 'the Month of Av.' The holiday—well, it's not really a holiday—listen, this is important—

Tisha B'Av is supposed to commemorate disaster, every disaster that ever happened to the Jewish people. Every destruction. They all happened on Tisha B'Av, the Ninth of Av. You see, it telescopes time. The first temple was destroyed on Tisha B'Av in 586 B.C., the second temple was destroyed on Tisha B'Av in A.D. 70. I think the pogroms during the First Crusade also happened on Tisha B'Av. And the expulsion of the Jews from Spain, in 1492. You think of it as 'Columbus sailed the ocean blue,' don't you, but in Jewish time, it's disaster. Probably even the Holocaust happened on Tisha B'Av—"

"Hey, wait a minute. That wasn't one event."

"Listen, can't you! This is my Tisha B'Av."

"Oh, that's just great. I'm your Holocaust. Wonderful."

"I didn't say that. Please. I never said that. But it's a day of mourning, just listen for a second. With all the prohibitions about mourning. No sex. No food. You can't wash. The men don't shave. And on the night of Tisha B'Av, everyone laments. They overturn the chairs, and people sit on low stools or on the floor. Like *shiva*, mourning, what happens when someone dies. They pray by candlelight, they read the Book of Lamentations. The Ark for the Torah is empty. That's what this feels like to me. My first temple is destroyed. My second temple is destroyed. I can't eat or sleep."

"Are you in mourning?"

"No, don't be crazy. Good Lord. Of course I'm not in mourning. But this feels to me like catastrophe. I'm sorry. I came here to you, and I'm falling apart, and I can't stop.

I can't leave you, either. Please don't let me leave you. Please don't go away from me."

(the apartment, daylight)

Blessed are you, God, who bestows good things upon the guilty. Who has bestowed every good thing upon me.

I don't for a second believe that anything lasts, do you? Anything about love, I mean. It could all be over in a second. A nanosecond. For no reason, for nothing. You'll get tired of me, or bored, or some universe inside you will shift and your molecules will tilt toward something else. Or maybe it will happen to me, I don't know. But when it happens, this between us will be over. You'll know it instantly, and so will I.

You said once that divine providence made you fall in love with me. You looked at me and in less than a minute you knew you loved me. It wasn't that I was so pretty, and we hadn't even spoken then. Not a word. You didn't know my name, and I didn't know yours. It was divine providence, you said, and I knew exactly what you meant. Some shred of divine grace streaking through the universe and somehow chaining us together.

But it could disappear, you know. Divine providence

comes and goes, you can't count on it. We might claim to love each other forever. But there are no guarantees. Divine providence just simply picks itself up and streaks off somewhere else. So don't for a moment think that I count on you. I never did, just as you never counted on me. Not now, and not ever.

(P a r t 3)

(outside, on the campus)

Nicole was sitting on a flimsy wooden folding chair in an empty, open-air pavilion, a temporary tent structure held up with aluminum poles set into the ground. It was class reunion time at the university where she taught, and there had obviously been a party here the night before: the round tables were empty but in disarray, the chairs pushed back haphazardly, there were blue-and-yellow-striped banners welcoming "Class of '84" and "Class of '74," but they were beginning to droop, the streamers that just last night had been billowing gaily in the breeze looked a little wilted, and the helium balloons were deflating. To the side of the tables and chairs was a temporary parquet dance floor laid out on the grass, where, during the phantom party, there must have been a band and dinner dancing. Nicole leaned back in her folding chair, crossed her legs, and clasped her hands behind her head as she watched her children. Jake and Caroline had discovered the wooden floor and were cavorting around, turning cartwheels, and trying to walk on their hands. There was a book lying in Nicole's lap, closed, unread.

It was great to be a mother, relaxed for a moment with nothing to do, watching over her two delightful children, at play, in the open air. Soon she would have to get up, corral the children, go home and put dinner on the table, look over everyone's homework, grade her own end-of-term papers. It would be a long night; it always was. But, for right now, Nicole had a moment to sit still, and she was very happy.

Suddenly the children righted themselves and waved energetically, calling out to their father, whom they had seen enter the grounds. David was carrying his briefcase in one hand and had his jacket slung over one shoulder; his tie was already loosened and a bit askew. The sun was beginning to set behind him, and he looked every bit the beautiful, tousled, and boyish husband, coming home to his family after a long day at the wars. "Hey, Dad," the children shouted, "over here. Come here."

Somewhere in the background a pickup band began to play, a ragtag student band recovering from that morning's hangover or warming up for another class party that evening. With only a few instruments, the band first scratchily played a football song and then lilted into some swing. Nicole stood up with the music, she just couldn't help it, and moved toward David, dancing to the swing. Forty feet away, David dropped his briefcase onto the lawn, dropped his jacket beside it, and joined in, snaking toward Nicole, his arms held out as if his wife already were in them. They met on the parquet floor, and without saying a word to each other David and Nicole slid into each other's arms. They danced beautifully together, as if they'd done it millions of times at millions of parties on millions of dance floors. When the music sped up, they jitterbugged; when it slowed down, David held Nicole tightly around her waist as she leaned into him, cheek to cheek. Their children watched, horrified. Jake and Caroline were so embarrassed that they couldn't take their eyes off their parents, who continued to dance, sometimes locked together, sometimes slightly apart, totally oblivious of the horrified stares of their children. When the band stopped, Nicole swirled away from David. He caught her in a deep swoon.

(a café)

Funny," said Jules, "I ran across her the other night, by accident. She was sitting in the corner of a restaurant, with some guy. Having a drink. From the back, I thought it was you, so I started over to them. Then I realized it wasn't you, but someone else." Jules leaned back in his chair, polished off his glass of Coca-Cola, signaled to the waitress for another one, and took a handful of peanuts from the bowl in front of him, all practically in one motion. He pushed the bowl over to Tom, who ignored it.

"Oh? Which night?"

"Let's see . . . Thursday, I think. Or was it Wednesday?

Couldn't have been Friday, she's at home for the sabbath. Must have been Thursday. Yes, Thursday." Jules nodded in satisfaction, having completed that puzzle, and then continued. "I was walking home from the subway after the lecture I gave at the Harvard Club, and stopped off for a drink, to unwind—you know, they run a lecture series twice a year. I should have told you about it, you might have wanted to come."

The waitress brought Jules his second Coke and looked inquiringly for a moment at Tom, who hadn't yet touched his wine.

"It wasn't David?" Tom asked.

"Not on your life." Jules chuckled. "Anyway, this time it's 'Theology and the Fictive,' see what I mean? Very cutting edge. Not for fundamentalists, though, so maybe you wouldn't have. . . . Anyway, my riff was the Book of Numbers as postmodernist fiction—have you looked at it lately?—an amazing work, competing voices, fractured points of view—"

"Someone who looked like me?"

"Yeah, but just from the back. When I looked closer, you know, clearly it wasn't you. Or I would have gone over, said hello. It was just another friend of hers. You know Nicole, she has lots of friends."

"Always has," agreed Tom. "So she tells me."

"Crazy how it's the big thing now, the Bible," Jules mused. "A real growth industry. Like the Holocaust—first a museum, then a movie. I wonder if you could make the Bible into a walk-through museum," he continued, suddenly lighting up with a new idea and looking immensely pleased with himself. "I'd do the conceptual work, you'd do the design. What a great idea! I'll bet the foundations will pour money—"

"Was she having a good time?" Tom asked casually, and then laughed out loud for a second as he raised his wineglass to Jules. "Terrible wine," he noted cheerfully.

"I'm afraid so," Jules answered, sizing Tom up. "A very good time, I would say. Laughing a lot. Very gay. You know the way she laughs, she just throws her head back. Nicole can be a lot of fun. Sometimes."

"Now, about that lecture of yours, on Numbers—" Tom cut in. "Interesting . . . fractured, you say . . . even someone of my persuasion . . ."

"You look a little fractured yourself," continued Jules. "Your parole going okay? Staying out of jail?" He leaned toward Tom, who downed his glass of wine in a shot. "By now you should know Nicole," Jules went on, "shouldn't you? That voice and looking like she can't take her eyes off you? The poor guy she was with looked like the cat who just swallowed the canary. Couldn't have been you. You're not that much of a sap."

"There's something to be said for jail," Tom said. "Isn't Numbers the one where God says he speaks directly to Moses, not to all the would-be prophets? Gets him back on track? Was she okay, do you think?"

"Who knows?" Jules replied dourly, although he was enjoying himself. "Why go into it? My impression is, sometimes Nicole just needs a little change of scene. She gets bored or something. She did look a little unwound, now that you mention it."

Tom wondered about that, about her being bored. He

also wondered if Jules would mind if he had a cigarette. He reached into his pocket. He had stopped smoking long ago, but sometimes the urge just overtook him, so if it wouldn't bother Jules . . . In fact, it didn't bother Jules at all; he wouldn't mind a cigarette himself, although he hadn't smoked in years and his wife would kill him when he got home if she smelled nicotine on his clothes. Actually he preferred cigars, but a cigarette would do. The two men lit up.

"Anyway, yeah, I talked about that very section, actually, where Moses insists he wishes everyone were a prophet. 'Lord, take this cup from me,' in your terms. He has that masochistic strain Foucault describes as distinctly postmodern . . . you know, the dismembered ego—"

"Nicole does sometimes seem to find it rough going," mused Tom. "Not anything serious, but, well, a certain strain—"

"Hardly," said Jules. "She looks out for herself very well, you may have noticed. But her, ah, *companion*— what should I say, her date?—her date was certainly drinking it all in. And she did something really unusual for Nicole. . . ." Jules paused, waiting for Tom to rise to the bait. Tom was silent, dragging on his cigarette and staring into the middle distance. "Really unusual," Jules continued. "She lost it for a second. Spilled her drink, knocked it right off the table. Takes a lot to get her that clumsy, do you know what I mean? Even from where I was sitting I could see her blush. Ever see Nicole blush?"

It was clear that Tom had not. In all those days of

stripping her, of watching her walk naked to the wall, of performing his will on her for the sheer, deep pleasure of her surrender to him, Tom had never seen her do something clumsily inept. She would shudder sometimes, when she realized what Tom was asking her to do, and her eyes would darken and go black as if some powerful drug had just kicked in, but she had never blushed. Tom rubbed his own eyes. He looked weary, drained. Surreptitiously he pushed back the sleeve of his jacket and checked his watch. He reached for his walking stick, as if he were about to leave, but then changed his mind and used it just to tap out a bit of Morse code on the floor.

"Were there a lot of people there?" he asked perfunctorily.

"At the restaurant?" Jules countered. He was still going strong, shoveling in peanuts, full of energy. "Oh, you mean the lecture. Yeah, yeah. A few hundred, someone told me. Really enthusiastic. A thousand bucks for two hours: an hour's lecture and an hour of questions. They didn't want me to stop. I could have gone on all night."

Tom tried to look appreciative. He remained silent, though, and leaned back in his chair, dragging on his cigarette and staring out into space. Finally he turned toward Jules.

"Jules," Tom began quietly, putting out his cigarette and leaning in toward Jules. "I hear that you've been planning for a long time to kill your wife."

Jules considered this. "No," he said, "but I wouldn't mind if someone else did."

(Nicole's office)

It was late in the day, almost time to go home, and see about dinner. Nicole was still in her office, sitting at her desk, a stack of student papers in front of her that she was trying, without much success, to read and grade. She would pick up a paper, underline a few things, scribble some notes on it, and then stare out into space. She looked tired, fatigued, and she kept rubbing her eyes; clearly she was not making much headway and might as well call it a day and head for home.

Jules entered her office without knocking, brandishing a newspaper. Without bothering to greet Nicole, he positioned himself by her desk and began, with a great flourish, to read. It was about Tom and must have been from one of the gossip columns in the daily paper. Tom had been seen all over town, apparently, or so Jules read aloud to Nicole, every night in a different restaurant, with his wife, the stunning, dark-haired wife who headed a well-known family foundation devoted to philanthropy and the sustenance of the arts. They had been estranged, as everyone knew, as the result of an unfortunate automobile accident, but recent sightings indicated they were back in business and cozy as lovebirds. Of course, continued Jules, relishing his reading and every now and again looking over the newspaper at Nicole to see how she was taking it, despite their recent difficulties, no one had really expected them to divorce, so deep were their financial entanglements and so mutually entwined their social partnership.

Jules finished his performance, deposited the newspaper on Nicole's desk, and left as quickly as he had entered, with a jaunty wave of his hand. "Enjoy!" he said.

A moment later he was back. Nicole was still sitting at her desk, exactly where he had left her.

"Look," began Jules, "I'm sorry. I shouldn't have done that."

Nicole shrugged, rose from her desk, and began gathering up her papers. "Never mind," she said, putting the stack of student papers in her briefcase. "Let's see," she continued evasively, looking around her office at her bookshelves, "what books do I need to take home tonight?"

Jules walked over to her side of her desk. Taking Nicole by both shoulders, he turned her toward him. Nicole stiffened and avoided his eyes, until Jules put both hands on her face and held her to him.

"I'm really sorry," he said softly. "What I really meant was—this is hard to say—what I wanted . . . I thought . . . well, what about running off with me? Somewhere. I'll leave Martha. You leave David. It's about time—"

Nicole looked incredulous. "Good Lord, Jules. What are you thinking? How could—?"

Jules watched her. "We should have done this long ago," he continued. "It was just fear. . . ."

Nicole was silent, thoughtful. "It wasn't just fear," she said finally. "It's something more like legalism—"

"Tom's not going to come through for you," Jules interrupted brutally. "He's just a two-bit architect with a rich wife and a love of the fast lane. You ought to know that by now. And David . . . well, you know what life with

David is all about. You've told me enough times." And then, more urgently, he added, "Now."

Nicole still didn't answer. She, unlike David and Jules, wasn't used to turning people down summarily, especially someone she cared about. She was used to shifting, changing position, uneasily, maybe, but her ordinary skill was to make small adjustments while the debris settled. If a building collapses, you don't tear down the only remaining support wall; you tidy up pebble by pebble for fear of dislodging the one stone that may cause the next avalanche. Clearly Jules was pressing her to learn something new.

"In the famous words of Rabbi Hillel," Jules continued, watching Nicole carefully, " 'If not now, when?' "

Nicole shook her head. "It's not about Tom," she said finally. "It's about my kids . . . even David . . . it's about marriage itself. Marriage doesn't end just because people leave each other, or even because they hate each other. It just doesn't." She sounded helpless, unsure, even though she knew that what she was saying, what she was trying to explain to Jules, was the truth.

"It could end," Jules said, "if you had any guts."

Nicole would have been the first to acknowledge that she had no guts, but that wasn't what would hold her back. She simply could not imagine the next step, the step after the massacre. She would gather her children and set up housekeeping with someone else? Especially with someone who had already drawn blood? No, not on your life.

There was something more, too, something else keeping Nicole from running away with another man, although Nicole, if her life had depended on it, could not have explained it to Jules. She could barely explain it to herself. It was just that marriage was, well—marriage. A sacrament. Something not to be broken off. Nicole remembered in minute detail the moment of her wedding to David. She was standing at his side under the wedding canopy while the rabbi recited the blessing over the cup of wine in his hands. He passed the cup to David's father, who raised it gently to his son's mouth so that David could take a sip, and then passed the cup to his wife, Nicole's new mother-in-law. Nicole had been fasting all day, as custom demanded; she suddenly felt weak and dizzy; her body began trembling all over, first her legs and then, uncontrollably, her whole body. She thought she would faint, faint from excitement and love and fasting, and only the weight of her long, white wedding dress would keep her upright. But then the older woman lifted Nicole's veil and gently put the goblet of wine up to her lips. Nicole took a long draft of wine. Her veil was replaced and she was no longer trembling, but suddenly tears of happiness streamed down her face. She turned quickly to David, and David, too, had tears in his eyes. He looked indescribably happy.

Later, after the ceremony, she and David had a few minutes alone in a room before the night of celebration, the feasting and dancing, was to begin. This time it was David who moved aside her veil and brought her face to his to kiss her gently, to kiss her gently again and again, and then more deeply and more deeply yet, in a kind of quiet frenzy. He loosened her veil with his fingers and removed it entirely, letting it drop to the floor, while he ran his hands through her hair, and they kissed in the first long, deep embraces of their marriage. When they finally let go, they held each other at arm's length and suddenly started to laugh, the laughter that is very close to tears, full of joy and anguish.

Now, with Jules staring at her, waiting for an explanation, Nicole burst out laughing, with laughter that was only a fraction about amusement at the ironies of life and much more heavily replete with hysteria, helplessness, and grief. She couldn't help it; she knew Jules would think she was laughing at him, but she still couldn't help it and couldn't stop. Finally, her laughter subsiding into moans and gasps, Nicole was able to get hold of herself, wipe the tears from her eyes, and face Jules directly. She shook her head. No. Finally, no.

When she didn't explain any further, Jules turned quickly and left her office.

Nicole gazed after him for a moment and then, after some hesitation, picked up the newspaper Jules had left for her and reread the column about Tom before stowing the paper in her briefcase. Whatever was she laughing at? The memory of David and how precious he had been to her? The utter craziness of Jules's request? How Tom was betraying her and would betray her again and again? She must be very, very tired to have come completely unhinged that way. She closed her briefcase and put on her jacket, finally heading for home, where she should have been hours ago.

But when she was halfway out the door, Nicole abruptly turned around. She fished the newspaper out of her briefcase and methodically shredded it into the wastebasket.

Gangsters

(voices heard through a door)

—I warned you, goddamn it—

—Don't you start in on me, you bastard. Back off. If you—

—Who told you you could take money out of that account, who? Now the mortgage check is going to bounce, not that it means anything to you. You keep your hands off of—

—I told you I was going to do it, I told you the other day, our other account is empty! Why don't you pay attention, for a change? There is no money in it, get that? None. Once I've paid the telephone bill, Con Ed, the garage bill, car insurance . . .

—What the hell are you talking about? You never pay any of the bills! You put your two measly paychecks in a month and who knows where all that money goes! Your boyfriends?

—Like hell! Who do you think pays the cleaning woman? Who pays for Caroline's piano lessons every week? Who pays for groceries, for God's sake? Every little glass of orange juice—not to mention the doctor bills, the dentist bills, birthday parties . . . Have you ever so much as taken the kids to the doctor, much less paid the bill?

—Yeah, big deal. You pay one doctor's bill a year. Look, you do nothing, you contribute nothing. Meanwhile, you've overdrawn—

—I've overdrawn! Me! Are you crazy? Who stole my
credit card and forged my name on it a million times?
Who? If I hadn't blown the whistle on—

—*I* stole your credit card? You're sick. You just have
to ruin everything, don't you! Everything I've worked for,
this family, my children, everything—and you ruin it. I
ought to— Yeah, go ahead, start shouting. Here, dial 911.
'Help, emergency, my husband's hitting—' Go ahead, take
the phone, goddamn you—

—Stop it, for God's sake! Lower your voice, you bastard—the children—

—Shut up, asshole, you—

—Don't you call me names, you bastard. I don't have
to put up with this—

—Oh, no? The hell you don't—

—You even try to touch me—one finger—and you've
had it. That's called assault. Now shut up! The police—

—So, call your cops, goddamn it. I don't give a shit
anymore.

—Shut up, would you. And lower your voice. Do you
want the kids—

—What do you do all day long, anyway? You sure
don't do any housework, no matter what you say, Ms.
Perfect Homemaker. So what *do* you do, what the hell do
you do? Study Hebrew? A little Talmud? Fuck the entire
neighborhood?

—You're right. I fuck the whole West Side. Because
I'm sure as hell not going to touch you, you son of a bitch.

—That's another thing—you never—

—You bet I never. And I never will, either! Drop dead,
will you? Do me a favor, walk out the window, just open

the goddamn window and drop out of it. Shalom. Sayonara. Good riddance. It will be a pleasure. With you gone, maybe there'd be a little goddamn peace and quiet.

(a café)

"I'm going to kill myself," Jules announced, idly stirring a spoon around in his cup of coffee. "Pass the milk."

"Oh, are you!" Nicole answered, pouring milk into Jules's coffee cup and knowing exactly how much he wanted. She seemed to find his threat only slightly alarming. Or perhaps she was thrown off guard and didn't quite know how to react. After all, this was the man who was going to throw her body over a cliff. One always had to be wary and suspicious around Jules; all of his friends learned that sooner or later, usually the hard way. She also, of course, thought Jules was crying wolf. Nicole herself had a highly developed moral code about crying wolf and would never threaten suicide without intending to go through with it. So why bother to threaten at all? Jules's threat was a sham, Nicole reasoned to herself, flashy, full of his customary mixture of anger, self-pity, and aggression and meant mainly to embarrass her. She believed that she herself said only what she meant, no more, no less, and would never use language as a weapon. Or perhaps the truth was that she had better weapons than Jules's arsenal of threats and self-pity.

"Why would you do a thing like that?" Nicole asked. She refrained from telling him that killing himself was an absurd idea; he was much more likely to take down some-one else.

"You know why," said Jules moodily. "And besides, if I don't kill myself, I might murder Martha. Or you. You never can tell."

Nicole inwardly congratulated herself on her astute-ness. So much for suicide.

"Now that you mention it," she said in retaliation, "it's probably a good idea, that suicide. I wish I had thought of it earlier. I might have suggested it."

"I knew it would give you a thrill," Jules said darkly. He held his coffee cup with both hands as if he were a child downing a glass of milk, looking suddenly so sweet and miserable that Nicole, despite herself, was touched. She reached out and touched his arm, stroking it gently until she got something like a smile out of him. He put down his cup and summoned the waiter to their table to order another espresso—no, make that a double—and si-multaneously reached for his briefcase, from which he ex-tracted a sheaf of photocopied papers. "An offprint for you," he said to Nicole, waving the papers at her. "My lat-est. An old-fashioned, lit crit reading of Moses' final speech to Joshua. Rallying the troops. A spin-off from that Harvard Club lecture I gave. Publish *and* perish, I guess," Jules continued, "but I'm going to."

"Thanks so much," said Nicole, taking Jules's article and glancing at the title page. "Where did you publish this one? Oh, I see, not bad. . . . Hmmm," she continued, looking abstractedly over the pages, "I see you're rather tough on Moses. I should have known that your sympathies would lie with Joshua, the young turk."

Jules looked pleased. "At least I'm prolific," he said.

"Going to what?" Nicole asked.

"Kill myself," Jules answered dourly. "They've already asked for another piece, the one I'm doing on the spies into Canaan. I guess they've heard I'm putting together a collection of my essays. Make a good anthology, don't you think?"

"Great!" Nicole said cheerfully. But she put down the article and looked squarely at Jules. He really was in bad shape. But Jules, miserable, would inevitably lash out at her, as indeed he already had. "With what?" she asked. "Kill yourself, I mean." She smiled demurely. "Just asking."

"You *are* dangerous," Jules said savagely.

"Possibly," Nicole agreed. "But you—you're a pious lad, and guys like you don't kill themselves. It's against Jewish law, for one thing. If you try it—"

"Maybe I'll use a corkscrew. What do you think—know where I could find one?"

"—and succeed, your local Sanhedrin will be on your case. They might even sentence you to death. In absentia, as it were. Ah, I see it now," Nicole continued with increasing brightness. "You kill yourself, some two-bit Sanhedrin will convict you of the crime of suicide, and sentence you to death. The first death penalty in seventy years! Suddenly—you're famous! The Jewish Rushdie! You might even get on David Letterman! What a clever fellow you are." She paused. "Too bad you'll be dead."

Jules stood up, took his article from Nicole's hand, and

stuffed it back into his briefcase. "Your turn to pay," he said coldly. "It's been a pleasure."

Nicole called for the bill and checked the available cash in her wallet. It was all right, she would pay. Treating him to coffee was the least she could do for a potential suicide. Jules shifted his briefcase back and forth, from one hand to the other, as Nicole juggled the check, her cash, her own briefcase. Suddenly she felt very sorry for Jules and ashamed of herself for treating him in such a cavalier fashion when he was so clearly in trouble. He was, after all, one of her oldest friends; she certainly knew him well enough to see that underneath his bravado and abrasiveness he was often shaky, untrusting, afraid of being demeaned. And didn't suicides usually announce their intentions long before the event? Shouldn't a threat, half jocular though it was, be taken seriously?

"On second thought, how about *not* killing yourself," Nicole urged. "Don't even joke about it, it's not funny." But Jules had bolted and was heading out the door.

Should she do something? Nicole wondered. Perhaps she should call Martha and tell her that her husband was spouting nonsense over a double espresso about killing himself. But wasn't it Martha whom Jules had just wished dead? Not to mention Nicole herself. That was exactly the problem: Jules couldn't inspire Nicole's unambiguous sympathy because the weaker and more miserable he felt, the more damage he was likely to inflict. She knew full well that he was the kind of friend who would come across you in some apparently compromising situation—on a bus in an odd place, let's say, at an odd hour—and not say hello or even for weeks mention that he'd seen you until he could spring it on you, when you least expected it, just to make you feel uneasy and guilt-ridden. And then he would walk away, chuckling to himself. If you were vulnerable, Jules would kneecap you; that was Jules. So it was just like him to threaten suicide and then bolt off, probably enjoying your confusion.

She should offer *something*, though, Nicole thought as she pocketed her change and picked up her briefcase, ready to return home and get dinner on the table. Even a few friendly clichés would do: *If you need anything . . . I'm listening . . . Would you like to see . . .* But by the time she got out to the street, Jules was nowhere to be seen.

(at home)

Hey! Nicole! Nicole!" shouted David, rushing into the apartment and letting the door slam loudly behind him. "Nicole! Jake! Caroline! Everybody! Where are you all?" He dropped his briefcase onto the floor and jerked at his tie to loosen it, all the while bellowing for his family.

Nicole rushed into the foyer from the kitchen, where she was making dinner, and Jake dashed in from the living room, where he was trying at the same time to do his math homework and play Super Mario Bros. 3 on the Nintendo. David had a big grin on his face.

"Good Lord, what's going on?" Nicole asked.

"Where's Caroline?" David demanded. "I've got something to tell you—all of you, together. Great news!"

"What is it?" Nicole demanded suspiciously.

"Just a minute, don't rush me, honey," David said, calming down a little. And then he bellowed again, "Caroline! Caroline! Daddy's home!"

"You'd better come in here," Nicole said to her daughter, poking her head into her daughter Caroline's bedroom. Caroline was sitting up on her bed, rubbing self-tanning cream onto her bare legs. Her Latin book was open on the bed beside her, and she was cradling a telephone on her shoulder. She signaled to her mother to go out, but Nicole signaled back to her, just as urgently, to get off the phone. "Daddy wants to tell us all something," she said. Caroline rolled her eyes and reluctantly signed off on her call, promising to phone right back.

"I've got great news!" David said exultantly, seeing Caroline trail in behind her mother. Then he turned to Nicole. "I've just won a nomination—well, I've just been nominated—you won't believe this!—just been nominated for an Emmy! For that documentary on performing arts in the public schools I worked on all last year."

"Daddy! Maybe you'll get famous!" Jacob yelled, jumping up and down. "Will we be rich?"

Caroline immediately caught the drift of David's ebullience and informed her mother that if she had to attend some party for her dad, she would definitely need a new dress, preferably the one from Betsey Johnson she tried on the other day, on the way home from school with her friends.

"Super!" said Nicole, ignoring Caroline's request. "Wonderful! Congratulations, honey. We're all so proud of you. That's pretty neat!" She still looked a little suspicious, but David was obviously telling the truth for a change. He certainly looked elated. David, in fact, was so worked up that he could barely stand still, and he certainly couldn't stop talking about it. The hype would be great, he kept saying, a real impetus for the new documentary he was putting together; it would green-light the teen mothers thing for sure, no problem. The children whooped around him.

"Come on!" he finally said. "We're all going out to dinner! Get ready, everyone! A special treat! A celebration dinner! We'll go to Marco's!"

"Okay," Nicole said reluctantly, but trying brightly to look enthusiastic, "but you have to give me a few minutes to put away what I've already cooked. I mean, this is sort of last minute, and, well, we were just getting ready to eat."

"I couldn't call," David said by way of apology, simmering down a little. "You wouldn't have wanted to hear this news over the phone anyway, would you?" And then, half turning to Jake and Caroline for support, he added, "I mean, this is great! It'll be all over the papers tomorrow! Come on, kids. Pack in your homework. First one to the elevator gets to choose dessert!"

(Marco's)

At Marco's, the four Wolfes were elbow to elbow at a small round table, Nicole and the kids with big bowls of spaghetti in front of them and David with an enormous platter of something that looked suspiciously unkosher like calamari. There were salads for everyone, soft drinks for the kids, and bottles of wine and mineral water for Nicole and David. The restaurant was hopping, even though it was midweek and early in the evening; Marco's was the best in the neighborhood, although it didn't have much competition, and a real neighborhood hangout. People were surging in, greeting each other, finding tables or not, sometimes just stopping by to talk to their friends. David beamed across the table at his family, obviously on top of the world. He was in great animated conversation with Nicole, shoveling in his food, passing bread to the children, all at once. A man suddenly appeared at the Wolfes' table and put his hand on David's shoulder.

"Hey, Steve!" exclaimed David, getting to his feet and pumping Steve's hand.

"Hi, Steve," Nicole said warmly, and the children echoed her.

Everyone shook hands, and Nicole and Caroline got kisses blown across the table while David commandeered an empty chair. Steve sat down—"Just for a minute," he said, "until Jenna gets here"—while David grabbed an empty glass from a cart and poured him a glass of wine. Everyone talked at once. Steve swung his arm over David's shoulder and said that it was really great to see everyone, and where had they all been for the last few weeks?

"I've got some terrific news!" David began. "You may not have heard this yet, my friend, but I've just been nominated for an Emmy! You know that documentary I did on public funding for the arts? Well—"

Steve was full of congratulations; David couldn't have asked for a better audience. But while David was filling Steve in on all the details of how he found out, what the next step would be, and so on, Steve suddenly interrupted with some news of his own.

"Listen, guys," he said, "I'm sorry to have to break in with this—you're all in such a great mood—but, have you heard yet about Jules?"

No, they hadn't.

He had killed himself. That afternoon.

Nicole's fork clattered to the table. "What!" she mouthed dumbly. Steve couldn't believe Nicole and David didn't know about it. He would have said something right away, but David was so jubilant that he just couldn't bring himself to spoil things.

"Oh—my—God!" said David.

"Shot himself," said Steve quietly.

"Oh, no," Nicole whispered in horror. "He couldn't have. You've got to be wrong. Jules doesn't know how to use a gun."

Steve said Nicole was right, Jules doesn't, or, rather, he didn't. It was a mess. "Blew his brains out on the living room couch," Steve continued. "Martha found him. She's hysterical, of course. I was just over there to see if I could do something, but there are cops all over the place, Martha was screaming at a rabbi, and someone's taken the kids somewhere. The couch is still full of his blood. What a job he did!"

Nicole closed her eyes. She put her hands over them, blocking everything out. But then she seemed to wake up, remembering her children, who were listening avidly. "Please, Steve," she said quietly, "the kids."

"Oh, yeah, sorry," he muttered.

"Sam and Jesse's *dad?*" Jake asked incredulously, finding a break in the conversation. But no one answered.

"Unbelievable!" David said, shaking his head. "That's a helluva thing to do. He was in great shape, too. His career was going great guns, two terrific kids, and even Martha's okay, really—"

"Shut up, David!" Nicole interrupted in a fury.

Why? Why? Steve didn't have a clue. Jules had seemed very morose lately, but when wasn't he morose? And who wasn't sometimes terminally depressed? Especially these days. Steve thought it was some planetary occlusion; everyone felt it. But suicide?

Then Steve's voice dropped. It turned out, he admitted, that Jules had told him well in advance, last week, in fact, that he would kill himself, but Steve had paid no attention. "I told him he was crazy," Steve said, "he had everything to live for. I even gave him the name of my shrink. Actually, to tell you God's honest truth, I didn't believe a word of it. I thought he was just being melodramatic. You know the way Jules is. Was."

While Nicole sat immobile, stunned, the two men had a very voluble conversation about what would come next now that Jules had actually done what he had threatened. Steve was sure, in fact almost positive, that there couldn't be a religious funeral, that no rabbi would bury a suicide, and that Martha would just have to make other arrangements, although for the life of him he couldn't imagine what they might be. David was indignant at Jules, even though he was dead. David couldn't believe that Jules would treat Martha that way, no matter what, on their couch, for God's sake. He wouldn't speak disrespectfully of the dead, may he rest in peace, but Jules always was a little monomaniacal. But as for a proper religious funeral, David had a dim memory from way back in his yeshiva training that despite the gun and everything, Jules's death might not technically be suicide after all. That it all depended on the Talmudic definition of suicide, and that, from what he could remember, from some tractate or other, for Jules to have committed suicide, that is, a *technical* suicide, he would have had to clearly signify his intention to two witnesses. One was not enough. So there very well might be a funeral after all.

"You yeshiva boys," Steve said gloomily, "you weasel out of anything. Suicide is suicide. The poor schmuck killed himself."

David admitted that Steve might be right, but a friend is a friend, so what difference would the definition make? He and Nicole—and the kids, too, he supposed—would visit with Martha right after dinner. He looked meaningfully at Nicole, who seemed to be in a torpor. But she finally nodded and said yes, they would visit. And in any case, David went on, this was a real cloud over his Emmy nomination. Mentioning his possible Emmy made David much more cheerful, so he went on to tell Steve, pouring more wine, how he got the news: not exactly out of the blue, of course, but, still, you're never really sure you've been nominated until you see the list. Like last time, for that documentary he did on American skinheads, when it turned out to be just a rumor. He should have won for that one; well, maybe this time. Steve mightily congratulated David once again, and David looked around the room, beaming.

But Nicole still looked blasted, immobile. Caroline even gave her a hug, which ordinarily she would never do in public. Nicole looked at her daughter gratefully for a moment. Steve, too, looked concerned. "You two were good friends, weren't you," he said sympathetically.

Nicole stood up. "I need a short walk," she announced. "Sorry, but I just need some fresh air for a few minutes. I'll be right back." Before anyone could answer or detain her, she had grabbed her jacket and was out the door.

(at home)

Luckily Nicole was in her own neighborhood and not far from home. She headed straight for her own apartment; she had only a few minutes and would have to get right back to Marco's and then probably go with David and the children over to Jules's place. So she would move quickly. When she got inside, she kicked off her shoes at the door but didn't bother to take off her light jacket or drop her pocketbook. She went into the kitchen, picked up the telephone, and dialed. Holding it slightly away from her ear, she heard it ring once and then she depressed the button. She sat down at the kitchen table, stood up, poured herself a glass of water, checked her watch, started to walk out, changed her mind, drank some more water. She was just putting down the glass and checking her watch again when the phone rang.

It was Tom, thank goodness, calling her back. She told him everything, as quickly as she could—that Jules really had shot himself, as he had warned her, that he had also warned the friend in the restaurant who had reported the news, and that now there would have to be this, well, this investigation into what exactly Jules had done and in what frame of mind. There was a religious issue, about suicide—probably Tom wouldn't understand, but she felt horribly implicated.

Tom understood immediately. "You're the second witness," he said bluntly. "If you confess, Jules gets tossed, right?"

Right. She should go back to the restaurant, Tom told Nicole, stay with her family, do whatever she had to do at Jules's place, go see his poor wife. But—listen carefully—she should not say a word to anyone. Absolutely no one. Not one word. She didn't want his suicide on her plate, did she? Wasn't her life full and complicated enough already? No, it wasn't lying, not really. It was Christian charity and the best anyone could do under the circumstances. They would talk later, he said, or tomorrow, or whenever, but right now she should go back to her family.

Nicole hung up, put her shoes back on, and left the apartment. Tom was a Houdini, no doubt about it. He was teaching her. Like him, she would walk away scot-free, whether or not she was guilty of pushing Jules over the edge. Or at least of not stopping him. She would be like those elders in the Bible who find an unclaimed corpse in the open fields, wash their hands over it, and say, "Our hands did not shed this blood, nor did we witness this blood shed." She would wash her hands of Jules: she did not shed his blood, nor did she witness his blood shed.

(Jules's apartment)

The day after Jules's funeral, which had been as well attended as any of the public lectures Jules had been so proud of, the four Wolfes paid a call on Jules's wife and two children, who, according to custom, were observing *shiva*, the Jewish week of mourning. David carried a large turkey Nicole had baked that morning, and Jake and Caroline were each carrying a box of pastries, bought from the local kosher bakery. Jake threw his box into the air and caught it while Nicole noticed and looked pained but didn't say anything. Only Nicole was empty-handed. She was apprehensive, drawn; she looked wound too tightly to have been crying. The rest of the Wolfes were in gay good spirits, David bearing the turkey as if it were the Emmy he expected to win, as if he were leading a parade. If his hands hadn't been full, he would have clapped the doorman on the back instead of just greeting him buoyantly and announcing that they were going up to 7B.

As is the custom with *shiva*, the door to Jules's apartment was left ajar for the mourners to enter, so all David had to do was shove it with his shoulder and march in. Nicole brought up the rear, semiclosing the door. Martha was nowhere to be seen, but Sam and Jesse greeted Jake and Caroline with noisy exuberance and then hushed themselves, remembering that they had just buried their father. Nicole gently hugged each of Jules's children but didn't interfere when the four of them immediately disappeared into a bedroom, carrying off both boxes of pastries. David had marched into the kitchen with his turkey, so Nicole had a moment to herself. She looked around warily.

The living room and dining room were thronged with people, huddled quietly in small groups. Everyone was either eating or drinking or both, balancing plates and glasses while they talked and milled about. It was no cocktail party, though. The mirrors throughout the apartment and even the ornate mirror over the carved fireplace were sprayed with soap or covered with a sheet. The cushions had been removed from all the couches and chairs and were strewn around the floor. Just as Nicole had said, describing *shiva* and Tisha B'Av to Tom, those in deep grief sit close to the floor. An older woman, probably Jules's mother, leaned on an overturned pillow, lost in tears. Another woman had her arm around her but said nothing, letting her cry. Most of the men wore black yarmulkes, either their own or borrowed from a small basket placed near the front door, and almost everyone had safety-pinned somewhere on their clothes a short, black grosgrain ribbon, ripped up the middle, to symbolize the rending and tearing of clothes by the grief-stricken. Nicole joined a small group of friends who nodded to her warmly but quietly; they moved to make room for her. Someone squeezed her arm in a gesture that suggested she merited special sympathy.

"Where's Martha?" Nicole whispered.

"In the dining room," someone replied, and then someone else added, "Be careful." Yes, Nicole nodded. She would be careful, she was always careful.

The dining room was even more crowded than the other rooms, and every available surface was covered with food. Turkeys, roast beef, platters of cold cuts, platters of smoked fish, baskets of rolls, were piled on all the tables. There were big bowls of salad everywhere, trays of cookies and pastries, fruits, nuts, candies—enough to feed the crowds of friends, colleagues, and relatives who would throng in over the next six days. A coffee urn was bubbling away, and one whole sideboard was covered with bottles of whiskey and schnapps.

The rabbi who had spoken at Jules's funeral was liberally helping himself to a large glass of Scotch, offering the bottle to anyone who would join him. David was at the large dining table, carving the turkey with much fanfare and the precision of a surgeon. It happened to be something he was particularly good at. Martha was next to David, fixing herself a pastrami sandwich and tearing into it ravenously. Ever since Jules's suicide she had been enraged, and now she was taking out her fury on the pastrami. David was talking to her animatedly, every now and again gesturing wildly with his carving knife. It looked as if he was telling Martha about his possible Emmy.

Nicole poured herself a small glass of Scotch and downed it in one shot before walking over to Martha. Martha let herself be hugged. "Oh, Martha," Nicole mumbled, putting both hands on Martha's tense shoulders and facing her squarely, "you are good. And brave. I'm so sorry."

Martha burst into tears. "What a bastard he is," she sobbed. "How *could* he—and what about me, and the boys!" David signaled to Nicole, behind Martha's back, to take the pastrami sandwich out of Martha's hand before it spilled all over the floor.

"He probably didn't mean it, you know," Nicole said lamely.

"Bullshit," Martha said, cursing through her tears. "If you've got a gun, you mean it. Everyone's always excused him, his whole life."

The rabbi came over, still with the bottle of Scotch in one hand, and put his other around the grieving widow. "Martha," he began, "maybe he caused trouble, but Jules was a troubled man. That's why, in the wisdom of our tradition, we have such stringent laws defining suicide. I'll say this to you again and again until you hear me: Most cases of apparent suicide are not technically suicide at all."

David took the bottle of Scotch from the rabbi and poured some for Martha into a glass, which he put into her hand. He looked as if he'd guide the glass to her mouth if he could.

"And even Jules, try as he might to make his death seem like a suicide, couldn't quite pull it off," continued the rabbi. "There was no second witness."

Martha thought, on the contrary, that there were probably hundreds of so-called witnesses. That Jules could never keep anything to himself. That if he had wanted to kill himself, he probably would have blabbed it all over town. She, of course, would always be the last to know. Nicole played nervously with her watch but didn't say a word.

"It seems," the rabbi continued, warming to the legalism of his subject and ignoring Martha's outburst, "from the severity of the punishments—no funeral, burial only outside the cemetery—that God calls down even more wrath upon the suicide. Today we would call it 'blaming the victim.' But, in fact, the opposite is true. Our rabbis, of blessed memory, have defined suicide so strictly that it is almost impossible to commit a true suicide. I have said this to you before, Martha. I said it at the funeral, and I will repeat it to you, and to your dear boys, until you understand. *You are not to blame, and Jules is not to blame, either.*"

Martha nodded. She looked completely unconvinced but was not about to fight the rabbi any longer. After all, he had had the decency to bury Jules with all the usual religious rites instead of just dropping him into a hole outside the cemetery. Nicole picked up Martha's pastrami sandwich from where she had surreptitiously placed it on the table and put it back in Martha's free hand. "Here," she whispered, "eat something."

Nicole chose a roll for herself and nibbled at it, wondering if there was any tuna salad and desperately missing Tom. She wanted to be able to tell him all about this: the sackcloth and ashes, the sheets draping the mirrors in the house, the sofa cushions on the floor, the mounds of food and whiskey. The bacchanalia. The fury.

"God is always on the side of the person who is troubled," said the rabbi, "and who of us isn't troubled? I don't think you should worry about this anymore. I'm sure that Jules has not jeopardized his portion of the world to come. God's ways are *not* unknowable, not in our tradition. . . ."

"We have to get going," David whispered to Nicole. "Here, Martha, sweetheart, more Scotch," he said, refilling her glass, patting the rabbi's shoulder, taking Nicole by the elbow. "We'll be back later, for *minyan*. Where are the kids?"

Nicole gave Martha a wary hug, said good-bye to the rabbi, and let David guide her toward the door.

(the apartment)

That's where you Jews got it all wrong," Tom said, "with all that talk in your Bible about cows wandering into fields and how much to pay if your oxen trample my vineyards. You *do* think God's ways are knowable. Just like your rabbi said. That if you come up with enough examples and definitions, you'll figure them out. But God's ways aren't knowable, they're mysterious. We Christians understand that."

Nicole was interested. If her oxen trampled Tom's vineyards, she knew she would have to pay; in fact, she had been paying all along, as had Tom. An eye for an eye, a slap for a slap. Justice, one way or another, was meted out. Still . . .

"God's ways are mysterious," Tom insisted. "You never know the price of something, you never know the rewards."

"You mean *I* might end up in the company of angels?" Nicole laughed.

But she secretly agreed with him, justice notwithstanding. She agreed that the ways of God are inscrutable, utterly beyond knowing. You will never know whether the person who stops you in the supermarket is a messenger of God or just some hapless neighbor wanting to know where the bottled lemon juice is. And the man in the white Cadillac who sideswipes you on the New Jersey Turnpike? Probably just some ordinary guy, a speed demon burning up highway. On the other hand—and you will never know—he could be the prophet Elijah, come with a mission beyond your comprehending.

In truth, Tom's insistence on mystery corresponded more closely to the way Nicole actually lived her life—not on the level of car pools, bank accounts, and homework, but in the fathomless part that had propelled her to Tom in the first place. And whatever had jet-streamed Tom toward her, the magnitude of it, the inscrutability. For both of them, it felt like the End of Days. But neither had any illusions about saving each other; in fact, they thought it was much more likely that they would destroy each other, blow each other up, in some way that neither of them could yet predict. You couldn't know the price. Whether you were saving a life or damaging it beyond repair, who could tell?

"If there's perfect equity, I'm in big trouble," Nicole finally admitted. "Look what I've done about Jules. I've lied to save his life. His life in the world to come, that is."

"Hey, hold on, wait a minute," Tom cut in. "I may be Christian, but I'm a quick study when it comes to the way you people reason. Your lie has nothing to do with Jules's life in the world to come, as you so quaintly put it. With or without your lie, Jules's salvation is determined by God. Not by you."

Tom was right: the price, the reward, you might never know. God works in mysterious ways. A man falls in love with a woman, let's say. A tiny fissure in the earth widens almost invisibly, a pebble slides into mud that will start the avalanche, a comet in the far reaches of the universe billions of miles away imperceptibly picks up speed, a boulder lurches from its position on a mountaintop. A twelve-ton truck shifts into gear.

Nicole had known that all along, really. That was what the apartment was for, the nakedness, the surrender—to feel the implacable force that had brought them together, to wreak havoc and some little salvation upon each other. While they could. While it lasted. Before it was taken away.

(*who? whom?*)

That was the only question worth asking, as Tom liked to say. But which of them it was who threw over the other, finally, was difficult to sort out. Certainly Nicole started it. She was even rather cold and rational about it, although she wouldn't have hurt Tom for the world. Even though she was ditching him—that was the only way to put it—she didn't really want Tom to walk out bleeding. She didn't want to wound him, not at all. After all, she loved him, for whatever that was worth. But it was over, the obsession was over. The chain that had held them so tightly bound together had relaxed, gone slack. What's gone is gone, as they both well knew.

It wasn't so much that she had come across him passionately embracing another woman; she had exacted her payment for that, and many times over. It wasn't even so much his wife, whom he was clearly still entangled with, financially and probably every other way as well—on those counts as well, Nicole had evened the score. In the vast and complicated arena of entanglements, especially marital entanglements, Nicole believed that everyone—herself, certainly, but also Tom, Elena, and David—pretty much got their just deserts. The wreckage evened out. So it wasn't the matter of justice or equity.

It was—just as she and Tom had been saying all along—that the finger of God pointed elsewhere. However you looked at it, divine providence was no longer theirs: He giveth and He taketh away, and that's just the way it is.

They were in the apartment when Nicole made her

pronouncement to Tom, as deliberately and thoughtfully as possible, because she certainly didn't want any fireworks. Not now. It was over, so be it. Fireworks—histrionics— were needful and appropriate only when there was some elasticity, some give, in the relationship. When it was over, there was nothing to do but freeze. And say good-bye.

So Nicole had come earlier than Tom that shabbat afternoon, walking unprotected through the rain and letting herself get soaked. She was waiting for him in the kitchen, leaning against the counter, her raincoat still on. Her hair was wet, and her face, the way Tom liked her. When she heard him enter, she hardly moved; she just jammed her hands farther into her pockets and listened to him close and bolt the door and shake out his umbrella. She waited for him calmly, listening to his footsteps as he walked down the hall.

When Tom came across her in the kitchen, he was a little taken aback, but he propped his umbrella against the sink and reached for her. Nicole didn't respond. She stood stiffly immobile, and Tom dropped his hands as if he'd been burned. He stepped back and leaned against the refrigerator, facing her in the empty kitchen.

Suddenly, although part of her would forever flinch from hurting him, she wanted to blow him up, blast him to smithereens. He had exposed her, uncovered her nakedness wherever he found it, broken her repeatedly, as she had broken him. So why be charitable now? Endings are like that, without charity or loving-kindness, without goodness or mercy everlasting. Endings are amoral, more so even than the love that chains lovers together.

So when she told him it was over and she was leaving,

at first he said nothing; then he argued with her. Then he said he might as well walk off a bridge.

She knew he wouldn't do that; he had too much to live for, despite his collapse. If stones suddenly came flying in his direction, she knew that he would put his expensive tweed jacket over his head and run like hell. But suddenly she was sorry—her sorrow was so desolate, so deep, that she couldn't fathom it; she had no words for a sorrow so profound, no apology, no atonement. She would have to live with her sorrow.

After that, Tom didn't bother to argue any longer. Perhaps he had wanted this ending all along. Nicole was, as Tom very well knew, armed. Dangerous. Often desperate. A gangster, in other words, and therefore someone to protect yourself against, someone to give a wide berth to.

Tom took his set of keys from the pocket of his raincoat and put them down on the counter next to Nicole. Then, without looking at her, he turned swiftly and walked out, closing the door carefully behind him. He had always told her he wouldn't look back.

Nicole stayed in the kitchen, leaning against the counter, her hands still in her pockets. She stared out into space, expressionless, not moving. She knew that she would never see him again, even though she was indelibly marked by him; she knew that neither of them would ever search for the other. Finally she reached for Tom's keys and pocketed them.

Before she left the apartment for the last time, she washed her hands. I did not shed this blood, she thought, drying her hands on her skirt since there was not even a paper towel in the kitchen. But then she told the truth to herself. Maybe because it was shabbat, maybe because she had spent the morning praying, even if it was to a God she only with difficulty believed in, maybe because she was about to leave the apartment never to see it again, maybe because she loved Tom and would always love him, she allowed herself a moment of piercing honesty: I did shed his blood, she thought. I was a witness to his bloodshed, even though I loved him from the moment we met and love him now. Suddenly she felt dizzy, frail, shaken, and had to steady herself for a second to catch her breath. It was the closest she had ever come to prayer.

(the end of days)

Nicole and Tom had once made a pact—that they would be together at the time of death—but even at the very moment they made the pact, Nicole knew it couldn't be so. Probably Tom knew it, too. The death pact was ludicrous, absurd. Each of them would be alone, or with someone else, but certainly not with each other. After a certain moment, whatever that moment was, when the universe simply changed direction for a nanosecond, swerved a nanometer, after that point they would be forever separate. Love ends, no two ways about it. It endureth not forever.

Tom would have said that only the appearance of love ends, that the deeper love goes on, it endures no matter what. In the same way that God's love for his children endures, unchanging, undiminished, without let, to the end of time. Consolation, perhaps, for Tom, who, except for a few moments in the spare honesty of the apartment, was only too easily consoled anyway.

But there was no such consolation for Nicole, much as she might have wished for it. She thought that human love, powerful as it might be, was not meant to hold a candle to God's love, whether you believed in God or not. God's love and human love were two separate realms. And human love was a mysteriously fragile thing: sometimes all it took was a brutal word, a silence lasting longer than usual, to eradicate it completely and without recall.

So when Nicole was unbeholden to love, at least of the kind of love that kept her chained to Tom, she was free, although that kind of freedom was not what she was looking for. Freedom was cheap; anyone could have it, for the asking. What Nicole wanted, what she always searched for and had found for a brief moment with Tom, was its opposite, the pulse of divine providence, the voice that said *Come, follow me.* The voice that brooked no denial, that you paid for dearly.

So she had gone with Tom, to the promised land.

The apartment would always be theirs, no matter what, unconditionally, even though neither of them would ever set foot in it again, even though each of them years later would writhe at the memory of it, remembering how totally each had surrendered to the other in those blank rooms. The image of Nicole naked against the blank wall was theirs, unchangeable, forever, Tom watching, leaning against the doorjamb, their lunch spilled around them.

The wine, the stories, the emptiness—all of it was theirs, indelibly.

The apartment would get filled again with other tenants. After all, this was Manhattan: how many empty apartments could there be in a city teeming with people, where a square foot of space can be worth the price of rubies? The apartment would take on a whole new life, furniture in the rooms, food in the refrigerator, aspirin and toothpaste in the medicine chest, books in the bookcases, children's toys littering the hallways, china and glassware in the cupboards. But for Nicole and Tom it would be forever the vision of the promised land, vouchsafed them for a moment before it was taken away. So however full of new life it would become, the apartment would always be theirs as they had found it. Empty. Full of richness, like the End of Days.

(at home)

Sometimes, late at night or very early in the morning, in the privacy of near sleep, she would pray for Tom. Just a few words to God asking that Tom not be bereft, that he might flourish and be happy. The prayer was anguishing for Nicole, but also a solace; it gave her a few moments, free and clear, to think of Tom unreservedly, to wonder about him, and to wish for him that he be canopied and protected, if not any longer by her love, then by someone else's.

But one night she also had a dream about him: in the dream, the phone rang and then Tom's familiar voice came through. "Meet me at church," it whispered, "please." That was all, but he sounded hoarse, broken, as if he had been crying. So Nicole dressed and rushed to the church, which in her dream was not the St. Stephen's she had visited with him, but a crypt of stone arches casting shadows on the stone floor. People knelt in rows, heads bowed, murmuring their prayers in the near dark as if over the dead. But Tom was not among them. She had come too late, or to the wrong church, or perhaps Tom had never been there, had never called, had never knelt and prayed to God who forgave all, had never said *please* or asked for anything.

After that, she tried not to think about Tom at all; it was too painful to think that when she had gone to him, even in a dream, he hadn't met her, hadn't needed her to come. But sometimes a memory of him would intrude upon her when she least expected it, when she was driving, perhaps, as or sorting the laundry. One evening, before dinner, she was at the sink slicing potatoes and washing lettuce for salad. Suddenly she thought of Tom; she was unguarded and he came to her unbidden. This time it was not Tom kneeling in prayer, but Tom pressing her to the floor, naked, in the apartment. It was Tom drilling her to the floor in utter, rapacious love, time and time again, until her brain was nothing but shreds of songs and flowers, until she was whimpering and whispering in shards and petals of language before then unknown. Standing at the sink, she heard herself let out a strange deep moan and then she was suddenly engulfed in tears, the knife still in her hand and water from the tap running over the lettuce.

Jake came into the kitchen, took one look at his mother, and threw his arms around her waist. "Mommy!" he pleaded, hugging her as tightly as he could. "Why are you crying?"

Nicole unhinged herself gently from her son, moved the colander from the sink so she wouldn't get tears in the salad, splashed some water on her face, and dried it with a dish towel. "I'm okay, honey," she reassured him, catching her breath. She leaned down and gave Jake a hug, holding him tightly for a moment.

Softly, so she wouldn't start crying again, she told her son that it was time for him to set the table.

(a window)

A little girl was looking out a window. It was dusk, but that quick end-of-dusk when every moment the light deepens and the air seems more and more fragrant, with a sweetness beyond belief. The little girl was very much alone, not sad or lonely, just alone. Her window was on the third floor of a large, old house, or perhaps a hotel, a white frame building that should have been repainted long ago. Beneath her, on the lawn, were the grown-ups, in a group, laughing quietly among themselves and talking, not paying any attention to the girl in the window, probably not even realizing she was there, leaning on her windowsill and listening to their laughter.

The girl was watching the air as it darkened, listening to the laughter on the lawn far beneath her, listening to the crickets, listening to the humming you can hear when all other sounds are stilled for the night. The fireflies were beginning to come out. If it had not been past her bed-time, the little girl would have liked to be running bare-foot on the lawn, catching fireflies and putting them into a jar. But she simply waited and listened.

After a while she heard the voice of a boy coming from somewhere above her. He was calling to her, asking her if she was there, asking her if she was in bed. *Yes,* she called out to him softly. She didn't ask where he was, she didn't ask if he, too, was in bed; she just waited and listened for him. There was silence.

From above, she heard the boy's voice again. *Say cunt,* it said. *Cunt,* she called out softly. After a few moments she heard the boy's voice again. *Say shit,* he said. *Shit,* she responded to him. *Say motherfucker,* called out the boy to her again, and now she waited a few moments before answering him. *Motherfucker,* she said softly. The boy called out to her, and she answered, she called out whatever he said, she chanted it back into the dusk and the laughter and the crickets. It sounded to her like prayer; she repeated it like prayer. *Cunt,* she chanted slowly into the silence. *Motherfucker. Prick. Cocksucker. Fuck.* The dusk was deepening. The night was getting darker and darker.

Acknowledgments

It's a great pleasure to thank those people who sustained me in so many ways while I wrote this book. I was fortunate to find the world's best editor in Elaine Pfefferblit. Her fierce intelligence and energy were gifts beyond what I could have imagined. I am happily indebted also to my superb agent, Lydia Wills, for her panache and her boundless creative zest on my behalf.

My family gave me invaluable support throughout. Special thanks go to my husband, Henry Wollman, and to our daughters: Lilly for her cheerful skepticism, and Kate, ever my encouraging and trusted reader. Rabbi Neil Gillman generously guided me in practical *halacha*. My good friends Lisa Alther, Ed Marston, and Diane Steiner read my drafts, lunched with me, and collaborated in my private chat room.

Most of all, I am deeply grateful to Robert Benton.